HATTIE'S HEROES

GINGER SIMPSON

ISBN-13: 978-1495937309

ISBN-10: 1495937305

Electronic edition of **Hattie's Heroes** published by:

Books We Love Ltd.
Chestermere, Alberta
Canada
ASIN: B007VEBEB2

June, 2010 – Kearney, Nebraska

Hattie's heart pounded and she eyed the rapid current. Terror cloaked her, but she dove into the river, surfacing with a gasp for air. Billy wouldn't have urged her to save herself for no reason. Churning water whisked her away like a dandelion fluff in the wind. She tried calling for help, but water filled her mouth, gagging her and drowning out her words. She craned her neck to keep her head above the white caps, flailing her arms and shivering from fear.

As the riverbed curved around a bend, she lost sight of where she'd last seen Billy. Death called her name, but she refused to answer. Instead, she managed screams of her own, so loud they echoed off the valley wall that followed the river like a curling snake. Her sodden bonnet hampered her vision, and despite the summer sun, the water's coldness seeped into her every pore. Kicking feet, now entangled in the drenched folds of her skirt, Hattie summoned forth waning energy, and drew strength from her growing panic. Clawing through the current, she drew closer to shore. "P-please, God," she mumbled through coughs and gasps. "Don't let this be the end of me."

Arms outstretched and fingers reaching, she grabbed hold of tufted grass along the shore. Inch by inch, she pulled herself from the river despite its attempt to reel her back. Exhausted and gasping, she lay on her stomach and soaked in the warming rays of the sun, her cheek uncomfortable against the pebbled earth.

From beneath her soggy brim, she spied shiny brown shoes, the likes of which she'd never seen.

St. Louis, Missouri – May 1840

St. Louis Protestant Orphans' Asylum

Chapter One

Standing in the dim light, her tattered valise in hand, Hattie Carson took one last glance around the common bedroom she shared with other orphans of various ages. Everyone else still slept. Soft snores and restless movements stirred the silence. Rather than stay, she decided to strike out on her own. Her heart ached at leaving the children behind, but what of her future. For once, she had to put herself first. After all, she was almost seventeen and, aside from staff, older than any of the other residents. The caretakers often questioned why she hadn't been adopted or at least married by now. Their comments stung. Having spent her entire life here, she now wanted to be rid of this place.

Others she loved slept in one of the other three rooms where fifteen beds lined either side of the wall. The orphanage had nearly reached capacity since the 1832 cholera epidemic left so many children without parents and in need of shelter.

"Some shelter," she muttered, reflecting back on the meager meals, hard work, and glowering looks from the attendants and teachers. Hattie couldn't count the number of times she'd been hit, shoved or yelled at. The only benefit to her stay was the rigid education she received, taught by a headmaster with a penchant for slapping students on the knuckles with a wooden spoon. At the unpleasant memory, she clenched and unclenched her free hand.

Her recollection of life began at the orphanage and included very few pleasant memories. The meager belongings she'd packed consisted of a second gray smock identical to the one she wore, another pair of stockings, pantalets and a chemise yellowed with age. The only shoes she owned were on her feet. She stared down at the scuffed toes and sighed. The paper-thin soles provided little protection, and she'd mended one of the laces by knotting the break. Would she ever own a pair not worn by someone else before her?

Hattie patted her skirt pocket where the three dollars she'd saved over the past five years nested inside a handkerchief given her six months ago for Christmas. Old Mister Cronin, the mercantile owner would probably be the only one who missed her. Who would sweep the floors, stock the shelves and put up with his colorful language?

By special arrangement, and because of her age, she was allowed to work outside the orphanage a few days a week. Most of her earnings went to the institution's superintendent, but she'd managed to hold back a small sum despite the temptation to spend it. Rather than succumb to the craving, she kept reminding herself that one day she might need the cash. Maybe the time had come.

The scratchy woolen blankets covering the sleeping children rose and fell in an uneven rhythm. Only her cot stood empty. Heavy curtains muted the early morning sunlight—the caretaker's attempt to keep the children asleep longer to avoid having to spend more time tending them... as if anyone in this God-forsaken place cared at all. A lump formed in her throat and she blinked back tears.

Leaving the children she loved wasn't easy, but unless she left she'd be subjected to the upcoming orphan train trip in yet another endeavor to find homes and ease the overcrowding. No one wanted to take in someone her age—ever since she turned ten, she understood how things worked. Now came the time to take charge of her destiny. She was more than ready.

"California has to be better than this." Hattie took a deep breath and whispered a prayer for those remaining behind.

A clanging of pots and pans down the hall revealed someone on kitchen staff stirred. Her heart pounding like a hammer against an anvil, she slunk along the marble-floored corridor, heaved open the massive front door and slipped out into bright sunshine. She eased the door closed and skittered off the porch and down the walkway. The chill that shrouded her insides melted away in the warm May morning.

At the corner of First and Market Streets, Hattie paused and fished inside her valise for a slip of paper. The murky smell of the Mississippi drifted up to meet her, and a steamboat whistle drew her attention to the river. How wonderful to be able to travel in such comfort and style. Perhaps she'd never experience it firsthand, but her spirits lifted when she unfolded the printed advertisement she'd found posted on the corkboard outside the mercantile.

Wanted: Responsible and caring young female to travel by wagon to California with a family of five—two adults and three children, two of which are twin infants. All expenses paid, meals furnished, and sleeping accommodations provided in return for assistance with the babies. Bonus at trip's end. Leave word of interest with Mister Cronin, mercantile owner.

Today, Hattie was meeting with Mister Franklin, the family's husband and father to gain his approval. Whether or not they picked her, she wasn't going back to the orphanage. She hadn't asked permission to leave, but her absence wouldn't cause a stir. Someone would take her place in an instant. Unsure what she would do if she wasn't selected, she nibbled the biscuit she smuggled out from dinner last night and resolved to deal with bad news if and when it came.

Her palms turned moist the minute she spied a dapper gentleman standing outside Cronin's. He wore the black Coachman's hat Mister Cronin had said he would.

Despite her churning innards, she closed the gap between them on leaden legs, and managed a weak smile. His tailored charcoal frock coat, starched white shirt and perfectly pressed trousers showed him to be a man of means. A thick moustache, broad shoulders, and angular jaw made him quite attractive, but clearly impatient if his tapping foot was any indication. A glance down at her tacky apparel brought warmth to her cheeks. If her employment rested on her looks...

She clamped the frayed handle of her valise so tightly, her nails dug into her palms. At least she'd braided her long, mousy hair and washed her face before bedtime last night. Pausing a few feet from the gentleman, she cleared her throat. "Are-are you Mister Franklin?"

"Indeed I am." One brow lifted as his gaze started at her feet and ended with a curious stare into her eyes. "And you're Miss Carson?" His uplifted brows showed his shock.

"Yes, sir, but please call me Hattie." She dipped her chin and took a deep breath.

"May I ask why you carry your luggage when we haven't even discussed what will be required of you?"

Fueled by determination, Hattie set her valise on the ground then looked up. "I hope I can convince you I'm the right person to help your missus with the children. I've had lots of experience dealing with young ones."

Fishing a watch from his vest pocket, he checked the time, and then cocked his head. "You realize this won't be an easy venture?" The timepiece's golden chain dangled between his fingers.

"I don't expect it will, but I'm not fearful of hard

work." A cloud of dust drifted up from a passing wagon. She sneezed—not once, twice, but three times.

"God bless you." Mister Franklin offered his handkerchief, but she declined to use the monogrammed square. "Tell me, Miss…uh, Hattie, do you have references?"

The lump in her throat threatened to choke her. "References?" She shook her head. She hadn't thought of seeking a recommendation, especially in her haste to leave before anyone woke. Besides, who would she ask? To most who worked in the asylum, she was nothing more than a face in the crowd.

"I assume from your dress what Mister Cronin relayed is correct. You've been a guest at the orphanage?"

Her heart sank, but she squared her shoulders. "Yes, sir, I've been there for as long as I can remember. I'm turning seventeen very soon, and an orphan's asylum is no place for a woman nearly grown. I answered your advertisement with hopes that by traveling with your family, I might make a fresh start in California, as I have no relatives to speak of."

"That is unfortunate for you, but I hardly think those reasons qualify you for employment."

She detected a look of pity in his eyes and lifted her

chin a tad higher. "I'm not asking you to feel sorry for me, rather judge me on my merits. If you ask Mister Cronin, I'm certain he'll tell you I'm a hard worker, and if the little ones at the orphanage could speak on my behalf, I'm sure they would tell you how much I've helped them. I assure you, sir, you won't be disappointed if you hire me."

Returning the watch to his pocket, he rolled his eyes and clicked his tongue against his teeth. "I'm not saying you have the job, but come along home with me and meet Mrs. Franklin and the children. We'll see how you get on with them."

Hattie picked up her valise and followed him, her loose soles slapping against the wooden walkway.

* * *

Mister Franklin paused at the gate in front of a large white house. "Come on, don't dawdle." He swung open the picket entrance and motioned her into the yard.

Hattie scurried inside, clasped her valise with both hands and stared up through the sheltering tree limbs at the balcony above. Rich, green ivy wove its way up the supporting columns and covered the railing. She lowered her gaze to the white rocking chairs and potted plants on the veranda and shook her head. Why in the world would anyone want to leave such a beautiful home? She didn't dare ask.

Fear gripped her. What if Mrs. Franklin didn't like her? What would Hattie do now that she'd left the orphanage? Her thoughts were interrupted by the opening front door.

"Young lady, please stop gawking. Time is of the essence."

She bobbed a quick curtsy. "I'm sorry, sir. I've just never seen such a beautiful place."

With the pressure of his hand against the small of her back, she entered the foyer. The interior was equally as eye-catching. Shiny wooden floors and walls adorned with pictures. She waited for instructions before proceeding further.

"Oh, Elijah." A voice drifted from the top of the spiral staircase. "I didn't hear you come in."

A blonde woman, dressed in a floral gown with a high collar and fitted waist, descended the steps with elegant grace. Slim but curvy, and only a wee bit taller than Hattie, she approached and extended her hand. "I'm Abigail Franklin. It's very nice to meet you."

Hattie ran her dampened palm down the front of her shift before she accepted the woman's offered hand. "Hattie Carson. And it's my pleasure."

Mr. Franklin yanked his watch from his pocket again and checked the time. "I'll leave you two to discuss the matter of caring for the children. I have business to tend involving the sale of the house and furniture." Stepping closer to his wife, he leaned toward her ear. "She comes from the orphanage with no recommendations. Don't confuse particulars with pity." His attempt at whispering failed. He donned the hat he'd removed, and with a touch to the brim, disappeared out the front door, but not before Hattie noticed a curl of disgust to his lip.

She gulped down a swallow and considered leaving.

"Please, come into the parlor and let's get better acquainted." Mrs. Franklin gestured toward the airy room to her right. Her friendly smile and face compensated for her husband's brashness.

Hattie stepped inside and gawked at the blue settee and the armed floral chairs. Their rich mahogany legs matched the table between them and the mantle above the stone fireplace. Nothing in the orphanage coordinated with such perfection.

"Please have a seat, dear." Mrs. Franklin's voice drew Hattie's wide-eyed wonder back to the center of the room.

After the missus sat, Hattie perched on the chair across from her.

"So, tell me why you answered our advertisement." Mrs. Franklin directed the question to Hattie, but nodded at the woman who stood in the doorway, wearing a white apron over her drab olive dress. Most of her graying hair hid beneath the white cap upon her head. She entered and deposited a tray bearing a teapot and two dainty cups and saucers on the table between the two women. She left without a word.

Mrs. Franklin poured a cup. "Tea?" She offered the delicate china to Hattie.

"Yes, please." Hattie grasped the edge of the saucer with trembling fingers and struggled not to spill.

After pouring herself a cup, Mrs. Franklin leaned back. "Where were we? Oh, yes, why you're here...." She sipped the steaming brew.

Hattie placed her teacup on the table and took a deep breath. Her insides felt as knotted as her mended shoelace. "I may as well be honest, as I'm sure your husband just informed you, I've lived in the local orphanage for far too long. I have no family that I know of, and I'm anxious for a new beginning. My entire life has been devoted to helping the younger children get used to missing their parents, so I feel quite confident I can do whatever you need me to do."

Mrs. Franklin rested her hand on her bosom. "I'm so sorry, my dear. It must have been horrible growing up in such a manner."

"There were a few bright spots, but not many. Aside from the love I received from the younger ones, there wasn't much else to cherish."

"Did you know your family before…?"

"No, ma'am. Sadly, I have no memory of them. In fact, I was named by someone at the Protestant asylum. I bear her last name."

"My, you do have a story to share, and one I would love to hear. But first, let's decide if this position really suits you."

Her spine rigid, Hattie picked up her teacup and took a sip. The tepid liquid had little taste. She returned the china to the table and sat back in a feigned attempted to relax. Her forced even breaths released the tension between her shoulder blades.

"Do you find the compensation for the position to be reasonable?"

"Oh, yes, ma'am. My expectations are minimal, as are my belongings. I assure you, you won't be disappointed if you select me."

"I believe you, Miss Carson, and I like your gumption." Mrs. Franklin drained the last of her tea and placed the cup and saucer back on the silver tray. "The first order of business is to make sure you understand this won't be an easy undertaking. I would hate for you to decide somewhere in the middle of nowhere that you weren't cut out for the job."

"Please, call me Hattie."

"Very well, as long as you call me Abby."

"All right." Hattie swallowed. "I assure you Miss Abigail, minding three children is nothing compared to thirty-three. I promise if you pick me, I'll see the job through to completion." She clasped her hands in her lap.

"I've interviewed two others for the position, but I find myself preferring your personality over theirs. You seem to be honest, forthcoming, and eager. I admire that. Would you like to meet the children?"

"Very much."

Hattie hadn't expected to shine among the competition, but her chest swelled with pride. Hearing she was favored by the missus made it hard to tamp down her glee. The veil of tension that shrouded her finally disappeared. She followed Miss Abigail upstairs, still amazed at the richness surrounding the Franklin family and wondering why they would sacrifice all they had to travel by wagon to California. A myriad of questions raced through her mind but prying into the family's personal business would no doubt be considered rude.

Miss Abigail opened one of four white doors and stepped inside. She nodded to the colored woman sitting in a rocking chair. "You may take a break, Tilly."

Hattie remained in the doorway of an opulent room bathed in sunshine, but stepped aside as Tilly brushed by her. In front of a small bed, a tow-headed youngster played on a braided rug with an intricately carved toy horse and rider. Glistening blue eyes filled with curiosity fixed on Hattie.

"This is Zachary." His mother ruffled his hair then walked over to two cradles beneath the window. "And these lovelies," she lowered her voice, "are Eliza and

Edwin."

Hattie entered and knelt in front of the young boy. "It's very nice to meet you, Zachary. I think you and I are going to become fast friends."

Her reward was a smile before he went back to galloping his toy across the floor.

Joining Miss Abigail, Hattie peered in at two sleeping babies. "How old?" she mouthed.

"Six months." The missus leaned down and caressed the straw-colored head of one infant. "This is Eliza. She's a mild-mannered child, while Edwin, I'm afraid, is more than a handful. Having two babies was quite a surprise, and I'm sure you can see why I'll need your help."

"Does this mean I get the job?" Hattie held her breath, hoping for the right answer.

Chapter Two

Miss Abigail smiled. "Of course you have the job...if you still want it. My husband and I agreed the decision was mine to make." Her throat wobbled with a swallow. "I'm really uneasy about making such a long journey... even if I didn't have three small children to care for." She turned and walked to the window, peering through the spotless glass. "Elijah's lumber business isn't flourishing since others have opened up, and he has his mind set on California, specifically Sacramento. St. Louis has become far too crowded with immigrants and the like. I can't argue with my husband when he only wants more for me and the children."

"More?" Hattie's mouth dropped open. The biscuit she ate long gone, her stomach rumbled. A heated flush crept up her neck, and she pressed a hand against her belly, hoping to quell the noise. "You have a beautiful home, servants, marvelous furniture...and look at your clothing. What more could the mister possibly provide for you?" Jealousy nibbled at her. She'd never been able to point with pride at anything she owned. Mister Franklin's decision to leave St. Louis honestly puzzled her. His wife's explanation in defense of his reasons bothered her more. Perhaps she was trying to justify them in her own mind.

Miss Abigail turned and faced her. "Elijah sees a need for fresh air, open spaces...a place for the children to grow and thrive. He envisions California as the perfect place. Besides, with the number of folks moving west who'll need to build homes, and the talk of miners needing lumber for their sluice boxes, this might be a great opportunity for us."

"So why do you look so unhappy?"

The elder woman took a breath. Her bottom lip trembled. "I'm frightened. I've heard it takes six months or longer to reach the west coast, and from what I've read in the newspaper, the perils of traveling the Oregon Trail are plentiful. What if we come across Indians? Or God forbid, get sick and have no doctor?"

Hattie hadn't thought of anything except escaping from her monotonous life. She knew little about Indians, but she was all too aware of the devastation an epidemic brought. Still, taking the chance was worth it for her. She touched Miss Abigail's shoulder. "One of the sayings I learned from a lady who cooked at the orphanage is 'don't borrow trouble.' Rather than fear what you don't know may happen, miss, why not picture a perfect and safe journey?"

Miss Abigail wrung her hands. "Fear or not, Elijah insists on making this trip, and I have no say in the matter." She released a loud breath and cocked her head. "So, after my cowardly confession, do you still want the position?"

"Of course I do." Hattie disregarded her mistress' fear and focused on the positive. "I've never been on an adventure before, and this certainly looks to be one."

A door downstairs slammed with enough force to vibrate the floor. "Abigail." The booming one word summons prompted panic in the woman's eyes.

She raced out into the hallway, to the landing and peered over the railing. "Up here with the children, Elijah. Is something wrong?"

Hattie hung back, out of sight and confused by the timid actions of her new mistress. Did she fear her husband? Discounting having just heard his raised voice, Mister Franklin seemed mild-mannered enough during their first encounter. Perhaps a bit impatient, but she'd put up with that trait most of her life.

Tilly, her skirts rustling, sped up the stairs and back toward the nursery. Passing Hattie, the dark-skinned woman kept her eyes downcast. She closed the door, leaving the hallway cloaked in darkness save one small window at the other end.

"Get down here," Elijah snapped.

Miss Abigail nodded toward the nursery. "Stay here," she mouthed before descending the stairs.

Although wanting to linger in the shadows and listen to the Franklin's private conversation, Hattie forced herself to open the nursery door and slip back inside. Blinded by the bright sunlight, she blinked.

Tilly's head jerked up at the intrusion. In contrast to her dark skin, the whites of her eyes minimized the ebony centers. She held one of the infants in her arms, rocking to sooth the whimpering babe.

"I don't believe we've met." Hattie walked closer and peered down at the seated woman and child. The baby's delicate features tugged at her heartstrings. "My name is Hattie Carson. I'm going to accompany the Franklins on their journey to California. I was informed by both Mister and Mrs. Franklin that I'm to assist with the children. May I ask why me and not you?"

"It be a pleasure to meet you, Miz Hattie." She bobbed her head. "I done tol' Mister Franklin I had no hankerin' to travel anywhere. I got me a paper that says I be free to make my own decisions, and I is content to stay planted right here. I plan ta work for the new owner as Mister Franklin says they be needin' a nanny."

"You mean he sold the house already?"

"Yes, ma'am, and everything in it 'cept the few things Miz Abigail begged to keep. He say they ken buy whatever they be needin' when they get to California."

The child in Tilly's arms began to fuss and root around like a piglet seeking a teat.

"This chil be hungry. Miz Abigail needs to come and nurse little Eliza afore Edwin wakes up. That woman be a saint in my mind." Tilly turned her attention to the child, holding the little girl to her shoulder and massaging her back. "The missus shore do deserve a more understandin' man than the one she got, but then I best keep the rest of my opinions to mahself."

Hattie stepped over Zachary and perched on the edge of his bed. The boy had fallen asleep on the rug, his toy horse still clasped in his little hand. "You can confide in me, Tilly. I promise I won't tell a soul. After all, if I'm going to be traveling with these folks, I need to know what to expect. I've already had my share of cruelty at the orphanage."

Tilly rocked back and forth, patting the baby in the same rhythm. "Oh, the mister don't be the kind that hit or shove you, but he shore can slice a person with his mean words. He be just like most men these days...always acting the part of a banty rooster, crowing loud and showing off his spurs."

"Well, that's a relief. I can handle words just fine, what I can't and won't deal with is anyone laying their hands on me." A shiver of fear trembled through Hattie at the memory of continued mistreatment by those who were supposed to protect her.

The baby wailed. Tilly laid the little one on her knees and jiggled her. "Oh, I do wish Miz Abigail would come up here and tend to this hungry chil'. Little Eliza is goin' ta wake the other two. What the missus needs is a wet nurse, but I'm well beyond those years."

The door opened and Miss Abigail walked in, her face ashen and tear-streaked. Her shoulders tense with worry, Hattie dared not ask what'd happened. Tilly rose, still holding the squirming babe so the mistress could sit.

Miss Abigail held out her arms, took Eliza, then put the child to her breast and began rocking. "I assume you two have introduced yourselves to one another."

"Yes, ma'am." Hattie nodded. "Tilly explained that I'm to be her replacement. Do you have any idea when we leave for California?"

Abigail's lips disappeared into a thin line. Her chest rose and fell with a breath. "Fairly soon, I'm afraid."

"And that's why you're upset?" Curiosity niggled at Hattie's nosy side.

The missus knuckled a tear away. "I'm more distressed over having to leave more of my beautiful things behind. Elijah is upset because he thought we had a few more weeks, but he received a wire today indicating if we want to join the next train going west, we need to be in Independence before the middle of the month."

"Oh, dear, and today is already the second." Still on the bed, Hattie's heels rested on the rail. She propped her elbows on her knees and cradled her chin in her palms. "How long does it take to travel to Independence?"

"At least two weeks."

"Have you ever been there?"

Miss Abigail shook her head. "No, this will be my first time, but I doubt we'll have time to view much of the city."

Hattie straightened and rubbed her hands together. "I'm anxious to see the wagon. I've only viewed them passing by the orphanage; I've never seen the inside."

"It's a good thing one of us is anxious." Miss Abigail caressed her baby's head and didn't look up.

At her employer's sad tone, Hattie thinned her smile. "I'm happy you hired me to come along on the trip, but sad that you don't seem more excited about it."

The woman released a loud sigh. "If I was sixteen again and had only myself to be concerned with, I suppose I might look at the journey a bit differently. Elijah has no idea how hard this trip will be for you and me."

"I'm sorry to be so naïve, but in what way?"

"There is only so much you can do to assist me. I'm nursing two children, and there will be times when Zachary wants his mother's attention. He's become quite jealous since the birth of the twins, but I'm sure at four-years-old, that's normal. Without the servants, I'll be expected to prepare the meals and do the laundry." She shook her head. "I'm not sure I can handle that much. In the seven years I've been married to Elijah, I've become accustomed to having people help me."

"It sounds like you really don't want to go."

"I don't... or didn't. Our life here fit me perfectly, and I haven't wanted for a single thing as Mrs. Elijah Franklin. But my dear husband fears financial ruin if we remain in St. Louis." Her mouth gaped and her eyes widened. "Oh, Lord, why am I telling you our personal business?" She cast a beseeching gaze at Hattie. "Please don't let on that I've shared so much with you."

"My lips are sealed." Hattie smiled.

After more discussion about her misgivings, along with a failed attempt to convince Hattie the trip wasn't merely an adventure, she settled the babe across her lap and buttoned her dress. "Of course the people who bought the house will be most happy to hear the news. They've been staying at the Planters Hotel on the waterfront, and the noise is horrendous. Besides, I can only imagine having two adults and five children in one room is quite exasperating."

"Are we taking a steamboat to Independence?" Hattie widened her eyes at the prospect.

"No, Elijah has purchased a Conestoga wagon and a team of oxen for us. The rig has been at the livery having the canopy covered with linseed oil to prevent water soaking inside should it rain. The process costs a little extra but Lord only knows what would happen to us without the added protection."

A flash of disappointment drew Hattie' chin downward, but a wagon still presented escape from St. Louis. Who was she to disapprove? She lifted her gaze to Miss Abigail. "Tilly tells me you won't be able to take many of your precious belongings."

"That's true. Even less than I expected after hearing Elijah sold some of the pieces dear to me." Sadness tinged her voice and clouded her eyes. "We'll only have room for necessities like food, cooking utensils, a few tools, and of course the feather beds for making sleeping pallets. The servants have already packed our clothing and the things the children will need." The woman glanced down at her sleeping daughter. "It's not going to be easy, traveling with an active four-year-old and two babies."

"I'm sure it won't be, but I'll do my best to ease the burden, ma'am." Hattie truly meant what she said; she only hoped she could live up to her promise. At first the trip was an answer to her prayer, but after listening to Miss Abigail, apprehension fisted in Hattie's stomach despite her positive outlook. Appearing tired and pale, the young mother had no sooner settled her daughter when little Edwin woke.

* * *

Miss Abigail put Edwin back in his cradle and buttoned her dress for the second time. "Come with me. I believe I have something for you."

Her interest piqued, Hattie left Zachary, now awake and playing on the rug with his carved horse and rider. He seemed such a good-spirited child and obviously found hours of entertainment with a single toy. Tilly took Hattie's place on the floor beside the boy.

In the hallway, Miss Abigail smoothed her skirt and sighed. "I never knew how difficult it would be to have twins. I'm so thankful you want to take this journey with us. I'm counting on you."

"Of course, Mrs. Fra...uh, Miss Abigail. I'll do everything I can to help." Hattie intended to hold true to her promise, but right now her insides fidgeted with the need to know what the woman had for her. Having received so few gifts in her life, she followed her new employer, niggled by curiosity and fighting to keep silent.

Her eyes widened at the luxurious bedroom they entered—at the huge four-poster bed, covered with a satiny spread and holding more pillows than a person could possibly use for a night's sleep. The one she used at the orphanage was flatter than a pancake.

A window seat, covered with the same floral fabric as the open draperies above it, caught her gaze. The room smelled of lilacs. She crossed to the window and looked out over a spacious back yard, puzzled at how much more space and freedom Mister Franklin wanted for his children. The small outdoor courtyard at the asylum paled in comparison to the vast parcel of land below her. In the distance, the Mississippi river unfurled like a ribbon toward the horizon. Steamboat, wagon, walking...nothing mattered except putting miles between her and all the bad memories from her past. Somewhere out there a new beginning waited.

"Hattie." Miss Abigail's voice drew her attention.

Her new mistress stood before a large armoire and flung open the doors. "Here are the dresses I've decided not to take." She ran her gaze up and down Hattie. "We look to be almost the same size. Pick whichever you like. I recommend the everyday ones since I'm fairly certain we won't have much cause for dressing up along the way." She stood to the side so Hattie could see.

Clasping her bosom, Hattie couldn't believe her luck. "Honestly? I can have what I like?"

"Of course you can, and I also have spare undergarments...and shoes if they fit you."

The lace around the collar and cuffs of a cotton pink gown peppered with delicate roses caught Hattie's attention. She pulled it out and held it against herself. "What do you think?" Excitement danced inside her.

Miss Abigail motioned to the mirror in the corner. "Look for yourself."

Standing in front of the looking glass, Hattie swallowed hard. She'd never seen so much of her own reflection. She spread the dress across the bed then returned to the mirror, stunned by the shapeless gown she wore, her childish brown braids, the smattering of freckles across her nose, and how ridiculous her booted feet looked six inches below her hem. It didn't seem so long ago that the drab dress hung down so far she feared tripping over it.

Alongside her reflection, she spied Miss Abigail digging through drawers in a magnificent piece of furniture that matched the dark colored bedposts. Never had Hattie seen such a splendid way of storing one's belongings. All her things had been kept in a bin beneath her bed. How could anyone bear to part with such beautiful possessions?

"Here." Miss Abigail held up a pair of pantaloons

and then went back to pawing through the remaining garments. She dangled a chemise that looked brand new along with a pair of pure white stockings.

Hattie closed her gaping mouth. "All this for me?" She accepted the precious pieces and hugged them to her chest.

"I'll step out and give you some privacy." The woman smiled. "Try on the dress and let's see if we need to make any alterations. Call out when you're ready."

The door no sooner closed than Hattie shed her depressing gown and yellowed undergarments. The chemise and pantaloons fit like they were made for her. She circled a few times before the mirror, still disbelieving her good fortune.

Now for the dress. She prayed it fit equally as well. With her back to the mirror, she dropped the soft material over her head and shimmied the skirt past her hips. Her fingers fumbled with the delicate pearl buttons at the wrists and the neckline, but she managed to fasten them. Holding her breath, she turned.

A gasp fluttered past her lips. "Oh, my Lord, is this truly me?" She stared with wide eyes at her reflection then remembered Miss Abigail waiting in the hallway. "You can come in now," Hattie called.

Miss Abigail entered. After a rather loud gasp, her gaze perused Hattie from head to toe. The sparkle in the mistress' eyes gave away her pleasure. "Perfect. Turn around."

Hattie pivoted then faced her. "How can I ever thank you? I've never had anything this pretty before...not in my whole life." The material felt smooth against her skin.

Her bare toes peeked from beneath the hem. Miss Abigail noticed. "Put on the stockings and let's see if any of my shoes fit."

Perching on the bed, Hattie pulled on the white knee-highs. With one leg midair, she glanced over her shoulder. "If I'm not being too rude, how did you come to have so many lovely gowns?"

Miss Abigail straightened, holding two pairs of lace-up boots. "My father and Elijah started the lumber business together. My father blessed our marriage before I even knew I was betrothed. When I finally met Elijah, I wasn't at all disappointed. As you see, he's very handsome, and comes from a wealthy family. If I could change one thing about him, it would be his drive. He's determined to make even more money when I'm quite satisfied with the plentiful life he's provided me."

"I'm sure it isn't easy to leave so much behind." Hattie pulled on the first pair of low-cut boots and marveled at the fit. After lacing them, she stood and walked around the room. "These feel wonderful. I have room for my toes to move, and the sole isn't loose like my old shoes."

"Then you may have them and the other pair too. I'd rather you enjoy a few of my things than to leave them behind or donate them to the church."

"May I try on a few other gowns?"

"Of course. You may take your pick as long as you have room in your valise. While you change, I'm going to check on the children." She held the doorknob with her right hand and ran the other over her left breast. A grimace showed her discomfort. "Edwin fell asleep before he finished nursing and I'm hoping he's hungry again." The door closed softly behind her.

Hattie stood before the mirror again and frowned at her braids. Before she tried on anything else, she wanted to see what she looked like with her hair down. After removing the yarn from the end of her plaits, she combed her fingers through the sectioned hair. Wavy brown tresses cascaded past her shoulders, front and back. Not exactly the style she wanted, but not the pigtails of a child either. Perhaps a single braid or a bun? She gathered her hair at the back of her head, leaving a few tendrils loose around her face. Better? She sighed. There would be lots of time to decide.

At the armoire again, she inspected the remaining dresses. She wanted them all, but ten were far more than she'd need. She stroked the sleek material then chose a sky-blue cotton with a tie at the waist, a light yellow gingham print, and a grass-green light wool.

Selecting the yellow one to try on next, she tugged the pink dress up over her head and found herself caught in the maze of material because she forgot to unfasten the buttons. A knock sounded at the door. Good, she needed help. "Come in, please."

"Oh, for heaven's sake!"

Her head still covered by the voluminous skirt, Hattie froze at the deep voice. "O-oh, goodness me. I thought you were your wife. I'm in somewhat of a tangle here. Can you please find someone to help me?" Her cheeks turned hot as a poker.

The door slammed and silence cloaked the room. Hattie backed up until her legs touched the bed. Encumbered by the pink cascade, she sank onto the feathery softness. Mister Franklin had seen her in her undergarments. How could she possibly face him again?

Chapter Three

"Miz Hattie?" Tilly's voice followed a soft rap on the door.

Hattie leapt to her feet, still tangled in her dress and feeling like a blind chicken. "Come in."

"Mister Franklin says you be needin' some help. I see he be right." Tilly's giggle enhanced Hattie's embarrassment.

"I must look like a fool, but I can't manage buttons in this position. Can you please get me out of this mess?"

Cool fingers touched her neck then drifted to her wrists as the nanny freed Hattie from the material. "That should do it."

Unencumbered, she whipped off the dress, lunged at the colored woman and hugged her. "Oh, thank you, Tilly." The nanny stiffened. Hattie backed away and smiled. "Forgive me. I hope I didn't offend you...."

"No, Miz Hattie, I weren't offended. I just not used to bein' so 'preciated by someone grown." She chuckled.

Although she hadn't seen Mister Franklin's

expression when he stumbled upon her, his stoic face flashed through Hattie's memory. Her stomach knotted with worry, she sank onto the bed and peered up at Tilly. "What frame of mind was Mister Franklin in when he sent you to my aid?" She blew out a loud breath and rolled her eyes. "I can't believe he saw me nearly naked. But, I thought he was Miss Abigail."

"Don't you fret, chil'. Mister Franklin be laughing at yer expense."

"How can I ever face him?"

"I 'spect he's seen much more than you hafta offer. Jus' act like nothin' happened. No use makin' a pillar outta salt droppins." Tilly clucked her tongue against her teeth.

"I hope you're right." Still fretting, Hattie rose and folded the dress she'd just removed. The incident hadn't been upsetting enough for her to back out of her new job. The thought of putting miles between her and the orphanage still made her heart race.

She continued folding her new garments and pondered Tilly's suggestion. Perhaps acting like nothing happened was the best way to handle the unfortunate situation, although she didn't care for a face-to-face reunion with Mister Franklin right away.

She turned to the nanny. "Can you bring up my valise so I can pack the things Miss Abigail gave me? I'd be beholden to you."

"That Miz Abigail be a real angel. She done give me some dresses too. Course, I had to alter 'em a bit cause I'm thicker in the middle. I ain't got much cause to be wearin' such finery 'cept to church, but I'm sure the good Lord won't mind if I look a bit better'n the rest of the women folk at Sunday service. I be right back."

Sadness gripped Hattie. She'd already developed a kinship with the dark-skinned woman, and regretted they had a short time left together.

* * *

Hattie awoke in panic. She bolted upright, her heart pounding like a hammer against metal. Where was she? Her mind spun, trying to regain her bearings. Sunlight pierced the frilly curtains and streamed across the floor. Nothing looked familiar. As her breathing slowed and her sleep haze cleared, the events of yesterday played in her mind.

Miss Abigail had hired her to assist with the children, at least during the trip to California, and insisted Hattie stay to help ready things for the journey. Recollections of her humiliating moment with Mister Franklin turned her cheeks warm all over again.

Tilly had been right. At dinner, Mister Franklin disregarded his encounter with Hattie in her undergarments. Dining with him and his wife had passed without incident, and for the first time in her life, she'd slept alone in a room—and such a glorious one. She smiled and embraced herself. Her life had completely changed for the better in a very short time.

Pampered by a feathery bed and covered with a soft cotton sheet, she reveled in the downy pillows beneath her head and the cool quilt that covered her. She propped herself against the rosewood headboard and savored the moment.

The room grew warm. She popped out of bed and over to the window, raised it and allowed a breeze to drift inside. Fluttering leaves on the adjacent oak provided some welcome shade against the summer sun, but the temperature outside already made her skin feel clammy.

She stared down at the street. A fellow on horseback, clad in a plaid shirt, black hat and chaps over his britches reined in his dapple mount in front of the Franklin's house. He dismounted, secured his animal to the picket fence and opened the gate. As if he suspected he was being watched, his gaze lifted and locked with hers. Mortified, she ducked away, her cheeks burning.

That one glimpse seared his handsome face into her mind, and she wondered what business he had with her new employers. The overseers at the orphanage always called her "nosy," but she preferred "curious" to describe her interest in things that didn't concern her.

Her stomach rumbled. Although she'd enjoyed a chicken dinner with all the trimmings last night, breakfast seemed a great reason to go downstairs. She quickly dressed, this time in the blue gown without buttons. Stockings and shoes on, she ran a brush through her tangled hair then pulled the mass back and secured it with one of several ribbons Miss Abigail gave her. The woman was too kind. Besides a rainbow of colored satiny strips, she'd presented Hattie with the silver plated brush and matching hand mirror. She had more possessions now than in her entire life.

Hattie glanced again at her hair. What she wouldn't give to wash away the crinkles left behind by her braids. But the most water she'd been offered sat in the matching porcelain bowl and pitcher on the washstand. Maybe before they left for California, she'd actually get to savor a real bath in water that hadn't been previously used by several children before her.

Tilly had described a claw-footed tub in a room called the 'water closet'. According to the nanny, Mister Franklin had planned to move the privy indoors like some "smart feller" in Boston managed to do in a big ol' hotel. Hattie couldn't fathom the idea. Would that horrid smell like the one she experienced in the orphanage privy take over the house? Those odors were best left outside.

Still staring at her reflection, she pinched her cheeks to add some color to her pale complexion then tucked a wayward strand of hair behind her ear. Stepping into the hallway, her eyes adjusted to the cloaking darkness as the sun hadn't yet breached the tree limbs outside the window at the end. The closed bedroom doors lent an air of mystery to the huge house. Her curiosity begged to open one and peer inside, but she tamped down the urge.

Halfway down the staircase, she stopped and listened. A strange voice added to the mix of Mister and Mrs. Franklin's. The conversation came from the living room. Hattie took a deep breath, made her way down the remaining stairs and stopped in the doorway of the sun-lit room. The trio, engaged in a discussion, didn't notice her.

The young man she'd viewed from the window stood with her employers. His thick shock of dark hair hung to his shoulders. Wild in places, his locks were obviously mussed and flattened by the hat he grasped by the brim—a symbol of politeness that impressed her.

"So, I should be here bright and early day after tomorrow to escort you and your family to Independence?" A southern twang colored his speech.

"That's right." Mister Franklin nodded. "And the salary we discussed is sufficient?"

"Yes, sir. More than fair."

Hattie cleared her throat. Quickly, she covered her mouth and gazed at the floor. She hadn't made the gross noise on purpose, but as a habit formed from sharing the dry night air in the orphanage.

"Oh, good morning," Miss Abigail said. "Come meet our... oh dear, what should I call you Mister Monroe? Our guard, our escort?"

Hattie looked up.

The smile the young man turned on her warmed the blood in her veins. She lowered her hand and managed a grin, her cheeks still heated.

Though slightly built, he stood a good head taller than Mister Franklin. The tanned leather chaps he wore begged notice. She'd seen them in the mercantile, but never on a person. In her opinion, they were a perfect fit on Mister Monroe.

The wrangler-looking fellow turned back to the missus. "Please, call me Billy, ma'am. I intend to be whatever you need me to be along the way. Since I'll be tending the cow your mister plans to take along, toting my rifle, and keeping watch at night, I suppose there isn't a single title that suits me."

"Very well. Then Billy it is." She turned her gaze to the doorway. This is Miss Hattie Carson. She'll be traveling with us and helping me with the children."

Billy bobbed a nod. "Pleasure to meet you, ma'am. I look forward to traveling with you and the Franklins."

Miss Hattie Carson? No one had ever introduced her like that before. At the sparkle in Billy's blue eyes, a lump lodged in her throat. The trip suddenly became more appealing. He wasn't the only one looking forward to the journey, although her reason suddenly had nothing to do with the orphanage.

Their eyes met, and she returned his smile.

Fidgeting beneath his continued gaze, she nibbled her bottom lip and searched for a reason to leave the room.

Mister Franklin, who seemed markedly quiet this morning, stepped closer and pounded Billy on the back. "Allow me to show you out."

He stopped in the doorway and glanced back, replacing his hat before leaving. He smiled at her and doffed the brim. Hattie's stomach felt like a butterfly collection had come to life.

* * *

Sitting alone in the dining room, Hattie finished her breakfast. The ham and eggs tasted wonderful despite bordering on cold from sitting out. The meal far surpassed the mush and stale biscuits she normally ate. She stood and started to remove her own dishes, when Minerva, the maid came in.

"Are you trying to get me into trouble? Clearing the table is my job."

Hattie backed away and fidgeted with her skirt. "I'm sorry. I meant no harm. I'm used to being held accountable for my own chores."

The apron-clad woman stacked the china and

utensils then exited the room without another word.

"Oh, there you are." Miss Abigail drifted in amidst a fragrant cloud of lilacs. Her light blue gown accentuated her small waist and full breasts. "I didn't wake you earlier because I wanted you to catch up on your rest. I doubt the trip will offer much opportunity to sleep in."

"I appreciate your kindness more than I can say. What would you like me to do to help? Should I see to the children?"

"No need to worry about them. Tilly is in the nursery, and she's having a very hard time letting the little ones go. I imagine Zachary, at his age, is going to miss her as much as she will miss him." Miss Abigail released a loud sigh. "I must say, I'll miss her too."

"I'll do my best as her replacement, but in the meantime, there must be something I can do to help prepare for the trip."

"Really, there's nothing at the moment. Mister Franklin has gone to fetch the wagon. We'll all pitch in to get things packed when he returns."

Hattie nodded. "I can't wait—"

The front door slammed. Miss Abigail's eyes widened. "That must be Elijah now." She left Hattie standing in the dining room.

The tension in the air turned thick as soon as Mister Franklin crossed the threshold. Hattie tried not to listen to the couple's conversation, but the raised voices in the parlor made it impossible to ignore.

"Please, Elijah, let me at least take one of the rocking chairs. When the babies get fussy, the motion soothes them." Miss Abigail's plea quivered with emotion.

"I've told you fifty times we do not have room for furniture." Mister Franklin's loud response made the hair on Hattie's neck stand on end. "The wagon bed is only big enough for the most basic things. We'll have to carry kegs filled with flour, cornmeal, other foodstuffs and water. The rest of the floor space will be filled with bedding and the trunks holding our clothing. Where do you expect me to store a rocking chair?"

"You're just being obstinate." Mrs. Franklin's voice crackled. "Why do we have to make this foolish trip? We've been happy here, and now you want to deny me practically everything I own and uproot the family. Have you even given thought to the danger involved?"

"How many times must we have this same argument, Abigail?" He sounded frustrated. "If we stay here, we're bound to lose everything anyhow, so we may as well strike out for a new home where I can start a new business and prosper."

"Th-then go without me and the children."

He laughed. "And just where and how would you live? I've sold the house and the furniture."

The argument halted and all Hattie heard were Miss Abigail's sobs.

Hattie jumped at a loud noise. She'd heard the same before when the headmaster slammed his fist against the desk.

"For the love of God, woman," Mister Franklin yelled. "Will you stop that insane blubbering and grow up?"

"Please let go of my arms. You're hurting me." At her mistress' distressing plea, Hattie hurried into the hallway, intending to run to Miss Abigail's aid. Instead Hattie paused outside the parlor and peeked around the corner. Cowardly, she thought, but she feared her sudden appearance might make things worse. Her neck craned, her ear inclined, she watched through the space between the door and jamb.

"You shouldn't make me so angry, Abigail." Mister Franklin strode to the other side of the room, then turned and yanked on the bottom of his charcoal-colored vest. His eyes beaded. "You will make this trip because as your husband, I demand it. Those are my children, and I will not see them raised in poverty by a woman who is afraid of her own shadow." He thrust out his hands, palms up. "What more can I do?" he beseeched. "I allowed you to hire someone to assist along the way, and I've secured Mister Monroe to help ensure our safety."

His wife stood with shoulders slumped and her gaze fixed on the floor. "I'm sorry, Elijah. I did let my fear get the better of me. I promise I won't cause you any further upset." She dabbed at her eyes. "What time do you wish to leave tomorrow?"

"At dawn." He closed the distance between them, gathered his wife in an embrace and planted a kiss on her forehead. "That's my girl. Now see to the help and make sure everything is brought down from upstairs for loading. I'm going to the mercantile to pick up the foodstuffs."

Hattie inched along the wall and back into the safety of the dining room, her nerves jangled. She'd just seen and heard a side of Mister Franklin that was all too reminiscent of treatment she'd already suffered. What had she gotten herself into?

* * *

Humidity turned Hattie's clothing into a second skin. She stopped in the shade and wiped sweat from her brow. She'd been helping the servants load the wagon for most of the afternoon and took a minute to catch her breath. The searing glare she received from Mister Franklin sent a message that needed no words. He'd done very little lifting and toting, but served as the taskmaster for those who did. Using her sleeve, she whisked the wetness from her upper lip and fell back into the line headed for the house.

Tilly, her arms filled with blankets, passed her in the foyer. The woman's eyes glazed with unshed tears, her bond with the children and her sadness at them leaving evident.

Hattie's tired legs trembled with each step up the staircase and into the nursery. Miss Abigail sat in her beloved rocking chair, nursing one of the twins. Little Zachary played nearby, but this time with a toy boat. Hattie's breathing slowed. "Is there anything else in here that needs to go?"

"Take her, will you?" Miss Abigail handed over Eliza.

The child squirmed in Hattie's arms, and for the first time, the baby's eyes were open. Large, brown and expressive, the little one searched the strange face of the person holding her. A smile curved the child's bow-shaped lips.

Miss Abigail tucked her breast back inside her chemise and buttoned her dress. "You may put her back in her cradle." She heaved a sigh. "I feel as though I spend my whole life feeding children." She stood and gazed around the room. "I believe everything that can be packed now is out of here. I need what's left until right before we leave."

"Then, if you have no need of my services at the moment, I'll go see to my own belongings."

"If you could take down the featherbed you slept on last night that would be a help. We'll all have to make do with just plain mattresses tonight because the wagon needs to be loaded with as much as possible so we can leave early. Of course, the regular straw filling won't be quite as comfortable, but we'll live." She passed Eliza's cradle and picked up Edwin from his. She caressed his cheek. "My sweet boy, I suppose you're ready to nurse."

Hattie left mother and child in the rocking chair and went to disassemble her beautiful bedding. She'd enjoyed a whole night of luxury and that was more than she could have claimed before. She hefted the awkward feather-filled load partially onto her left shoulder but mostly on her head. She stumbled back beneath the weight, but regained her balance. Whoever said "light as a feather" never carried a bunch of them at once.

Praying she wouldn't fall down the stairs, step-by-step, she clung with one hand to the banister. She'd just reached the bottom when she saw a pair of booted feet. Someone lifted her burden.

"Let me get that for you, Miss Carson." She recognized the voice and froze as her gaze followed Billy Monroe out the door.

Grasping her stomach, she closed her gaping mouth. She must look a sight—her hair a mess and her clothing wrinkled and sticky. Where had he come from? He wasn't supposed to show up until early tomorrow morning.

Before he returned, she scrambled up the stairs, into her room and took her brush and mirror from her valise. Maybe he hadn't gotten a good look at her disheveled state. She pulled the brush through her damp locks and pondered her strange reaction to Mister Billy Monroe. What confused her more than his being at the

Franklin's already was why she cared? Seeing him did funny things to her innards and she couldn't begin to explain why.

Chapter Four

Hattie stood in the living room shadows and watched Billy from the window. His bare arms and shoulders tensed beneath the weight of the crates and boxes he hefted over the wagon's tailgate. His skin glistened with sweat. When he climbed into the Conestoga, she sashayed out the front door, feeling more presentable with her hair brushed and secured at her neck with a lavender ribbon. She followed the path of crushed grass to the wagon and peered in while he arranged the load. The nearness of him turned her mouth dry as cotton, and she had no idea what to say.

Her pulse quickened when he turned and noticed her.

"Good day, Miss Carson." His dimpled smile stole the air from her lungs. "From the looks of things, everyone has been busy today."

Despite the midday heat, goose bumps dotted her arms. She smiled and swallowed the nervous lump in her throat. "I-I didn't expect to see you until tomorrow."

He moved closer to the opening of the wagon's white canvas bonnet and peered down. "Mister Franklin came by the boardin' house and asked me to start work today. Since everything is bein' loaded, he said he'd feel a lot safer if I slept in the wagon overnight."

Craning her neck caused a cramp. Hattie stepped back and gazed up beneath a hand shielding her eyes from the sun. "I suppose that makes sense. One can never be too careful." She ran damp palms down her skirt then twined her fingers in the cotton folds. In the past, food she'd saved from orphanage meals and stashed away to stave off nighttime hunger disappeared from beneath her bed despite all the children in the orphanage being forced to recite the Lord's commandments every day. Thievery was thievery, plain and simple. No telling who was trustworthy these days.

"Is there anything I can help bring down to the wagon, Miss Hattie?" Billy's offer interrupted her thoughts.

An image of him toting her down the stairs in those strong arms flashed in her mind, sending warmth creeping along her neck. "O-oh...no, thank you. I have only a valise, and I'll need my things in the morning. I think everything else has been loaded."

"In that case, I'll take care of one last errand at the mercantile for Mister Franklin. Seems he forgot to pick up grease for the wagon wheels and some extra rope." Billy vaulted over the tailgate and landed with a thud next to her. He retrieved his shirt from the nearest wheel and began buttoning. "Do you need anything while I'm shopping?"

He smelled of leather, soap and sweat—a stirring combination, and his closeness made her heart beat faster. Lost in the confusion of her raging emotions, she shook her head.

"I'll be back as soon as I can." He removed his hat and ran his fingers through the damp curls beneath it. "If Mister Franklin asks where I've gone, please tell him, won't you?" He plopped his hat back in place and tugged the brim low over his brow.

Like a mute, she nodded, but managed a smile. Her gaze followed him to his horse. Billy placed a booted foot in the stirrup and swung the other long leg over the animal's back with ease. She admired his strength and the way his hair tickled his collar and curled at his neck's nape. All the boys she'd been around before were much younger and a whole lot less interesting.

She realized she stared when Billy tipped his hat before he rode away. She lowered her head and bit her knuckle. What about him made her look at him like a hungry calf trailing its momma? What must he think?

"Hattie." Miss Abigail's voice beckoned from the parlor window. "Can you please join me?"

Hiking up her skirt hem, Hattie hurried inside. She stepped into the room, paused and took a breath. Should she explain she'd been helping Billy and not dawdling? She decided to say nothing and bobbed a curtsy. "Yes, ma'am."

Miss Abigail turned from the window and crossed to the settee. She sat and patted the cushion next to her. "Come sit. I'd like to talk to you."

Dread mingled with fear in Hattie's heart. Was she going to be discharged without even having a chance to demonstrate her talent with children? And where was Mister Franklin? His scowls and piercing stares had already hinted he had no use for her—as if she might be a slacker. Hadn't she'd done more than her share this morning?

Hattie scanned the hallway and then looked back at Miss Abigail. "Have I done something to displease the mister?"

"Elijah's gone to the lumber mill to settle his final

business there." His wife clucked her tongue against her teeth. "And don't fret. He already told me how glad he is I hired you."

"Really, ma'am?" Hattie inched forward, her mouth agape. "He sure does paint a whole other picture with his actions. I don't mind telling you, Miss Abigail, I'm not very brave when it comes to men. Suppose it's cause I haven't been around very many in my life."

Her mistress patted the seat next to her again and smiled. "Elijah may seem gruff, but most of the time he's kind-hearted and caring. You've only seen the side of him that's disappointed at having to sell a business he and his father started together."

Hattie sat and clasped her hands in her lap. She turned toward Miss Abigail, bumping knees with her. "I hope you won't be angry with me for butting into your business, but he raised his voice at you in this very room. I heard you cry."

The woman's cheeks turned red. "Oh, that was my fault. I should never have pressed the issue of the move at this late date. Elijah did everything he could to avoid uprooting the family, but as I told you, he wants only the best for us, and he fears we'll lose what we have here.

Besides, he apologized over and over last night before we went to sleep."

Lowering her gaze, Hattie stared into her lap. "I shouldn't have been eavesdropping—"

"Pshaw." Miss Abigail flicked a dismissing wave. "How could you not hear Elijah's booming voice? If you plan to travel with us for the next five or six months, then you'd best get used to his ranting. He does tend to get loud when things don't go his way."

"Five or six months? Is that how long it takes to get to California?" The length of time surprised her more than Mister Franklin's temper.

"So I've been told... and that's starting from Independence. Elijah says we've joined the last wagon train leaving this year for the west, but I admit I wish we'd have missed it. I'm frightened."

"I'm sure the trail master knows the dangers well."

"I certainly hope you're right, Hattie. I've had conversations with those who have made the trip from the west. One of the biggest dangers is drowning. There are so many rivers to cross and no one ever knows how fast the flow or how deep the water. I'm not worried for myself as much as I am for my children."

Finding out it would take months to reach their destination and hearing her mistress speak of her fears caused clouds of apprehension to gather in Hattie's mind. The trip wouldn't be the quick, easy one she believed, despite the distance to be traveled looking much shorter on the map in the orphanage classroom.

She fidgeted with her fingers and sought something positive to calm the mistress' nerves. Feigning a confident smile, she glanced up. "B-But think of how many have gone before us. If traveling proved too dangerous, I don't believe anyone would follow in their footsteps."

Miss Abigail twisted a handkerchief into knots. "Even though the wagon is stocked for the journey, who knows how long the food supplies will last? Is there enough cornmeal and dried meat? I suppose we'll find out." The woman's brow furrowed. "Now that Mister Monroe is coming along, we'll be feeding yet another mouth."

"I'm sure there are mercantiles along the way where supplies can be replaced." Hattie refused to be negative.

Miss Abigail shuddered and shook her head. "Oh, the thought of what lies ahead is far too overwhelming to consider." She straightened and leaned back. "The trip's peril isn't what I wanted to talk to you about."

"What then?"

"I know it seems I've been far too personal with you given you're in my employ, but you so remind me of my younger sister."

"I do? Does she live nearby? Is she going to California too?" At the thought of a friend her own age, excitement surged through Hattie...until she saw Miss Abigail's throat wobble with a hard swallow.

"Missy passed from smallpox a few years back."

"Oh, I-I'm so sorry." Hattie clamped her lips together, wishing she had better control of her curious side.

"There's no need to apologize, my dear. I'm sure my sweet sister is in a better place now. I wanted you to know I find comfort in having you here, and I would really like you to call me Abby."

"You won't think me forward?" Hattie cocked her head.

"I made the request, so how could I think that of you?" Miss Abigail giggled. "I also have a few things of Missy's I've kept, and I'd like you to have them: a few bonnets and her Bible. I think both might prove very useful during the next months."

Moved to tears by the woman's thoughtful gesture, Hattie blotted her eyes. She'd never been treated with such kindness. "I don't know what to say but—"

Abby touched her index finger to Hattie's lips. "There's no need to say more. I've left your new things on the bed where you slept last night."

* * *

Sadness lingered in the dining room like fog shrouding the ol' Mississippi. For this special occasion, Abigail invited Tilly to join the family for their last dinner in St. Louis. While she ate, her red-rimmed gaze remained on little Zachary, and she frequently reached over and stroked his arm. The child looked at her with adoring eyes—a look Hattie wondered if she might ever receive. The stoic maid, who had barked earlier at Hattie for daring to remove her dirty dishes from the table, refilled glasses and cups, her lips pulled into a thin line, her eyes brimming with unshed tears.

The tinkling of silverware against the china and an occasional sigh were the only sounds that cut the silence. Despite the dreary atmosphere, Hattie savored the fried chicken and collard greens, thankful for real food instead of the dreadful mush served daily at the orphanage. While chewing, she glanced at Abby, who stared into her plate and toyed with her fork. Making the journey would be difficult for someone as fragile as the missus, but Hattie remained determined to lighten the woman's load as much as possible. Who wouldn't feel a kinship with such a kindhearted woman?

Hattie's thoughts drifted to Billy Monroe. Why hadn't they invited him to dinner? Surely he was hungry and would like some fried chicken. Several pieces remained.

The sound of Mister Franklin's chair scraping back from the table jostled Hattie from her planned chicken thievery. Her employer reached over his head with one hand in a long stretch and patted his stomach with the other. "Tasty dinner, I must say." Reaching inside his beige jacket, he took out a fat cigar.

The maid scurried over with a match. Mister Franklin struck it against the sole of his boot and then lit the rolled tobacco. The cigar's end burned bright red as he inhaled. Smoke furled upward, and an unpleasant odor drifted across the table. Hattie wrinkled her nose and put down her fork. Her first experience with someone smoking at the table ruined what was left of her appetite.

"Why does everyone look as though someone

died?" Mister Franklin asked.

Abby lifted her chin and met his gaze. "The mood is called sadness, Elijah." Sarcasm iced her voice. "I'm sorry, but despite all our conversations about the trip, I'm still going to miss Tilly and the others who have worked for us for so long."

"Yes, my dear, I realize that. I, too, shall miss them, but rest assured the new owners will retain her and the rest. Plus, I've given each who worked for us a generous bonus for their dedication."

Not wanting to involve herself in personal business, Hattie removed the napkin from her lap and draped it across her almost empty plate. "May I be excused?"

"Of course, you may," Abby answered. "I think we should all excuse ourselves and get ready for bed. We have an early start tomorrow."

Hattie eyed the remaining chicken again. "Would you mind if I took a piece of chicken to Mister Monroe? I'm sure he would enjoy it."

"Please, take him two." Abby rose and pushed in her chair. "Tilly, would you please get Zachary ready for bed? I'm going to see to the babies."

Grabbing an unused dinner napkin, Hattie wrapped

a chicken leg and thigh inside and hurried out of the dining room.

* * *

Hattie stepped out into the balmy summer evening, carrying the napkin warmed by the chicken inside. The crickets' vibrating song filled the air, but fell silent when her footfall threatened approach. Pinpoints of light drifted upward from fireflies dancing in the grass. The festive show never failed to amaze her.

Slivers of light filtered through the trees and lit her way to the wagon parked in front of the house. The tailgate was down, and Billy's horse stood tethered to a peg. Illumination inside created an occasional shadow across the fabric.

"Mister Monroe," she called, having no desire to breech his privacy. "I've brought you something."

The four oxen tethered to a nearby oak munched noisily on the grass at their feet. Only one cast a slight sideways glance at hearing Hattie's voice.

Billy stepped out onto the wooden platform. Shirtless again, he looked down at her and smiled. "I hope it's something to eat. The biscuit and hardtack I had earlier didn't quell my hunger."

Her cheeks grew hot at seeing so much bare skin again. She lowered her gaze and handed him the bundle. "It's fried chicken. Miss Abigail gave me permission to bring you some." Averting her eyes did little to erase the image of his muscled arms and the fine hair dotting his chest. Did Billy Monroe ever wear a shirt for very long?

CHAPTER FIVE

Billy realized Hattie's discomfort and snagged his shirt from atop one of the kegs inside the wagon. "I-I was just about to blow out the lamp and go to sleep." He slipped his arms inside the sleeves but didn't bother to button up.

Plopping on the tailgate, he dangled his legs over the edge and unwrapped the napkin. The aroma of fried chicken wafted in the air. "I declare, this looks good and smells even better." He patted the place next to him. "Won't you sit with me while I eat?"

She lifted her chin a bit. "Maybe just for a minute." Her failed attempt to hop onto the tailgate left her teetering on the edge.

"Whoa." Billy grabbed her arm and steadied her with one hand, and held his meal with the other. Without another word, he ripped a chunk of meat from the drumstick with his teeth and chewed.

Hattie swung her feet back and forth in rhythm with his bare ones and stared down the street. "Have you ever been west?"

"Uh huh." He swallowed and nodded. "Been all the way to California before with another wagon train."

Her head snapped around, her eyes wide. "Really? You're so young."

"No bull, I really been there, and I ain't so young. I'm twenty already." He took another bite then swiped his sleeve across his chin. The sheen of grease disappeared.

There wasn't such a difference in their ages, but now wasn't the time for that discussion. "You know, Miss Abigail is really frightened over this trip. Maybe you could share some things to make her feel better." The cock of her head and her serious tone gave him pause.

He re-wrapped the second piece of chicken, along with the bones from the first, laid the napkin aside and ran his greasy palms down his pant leg. "I'm not sure anything I can tell her will ease her worry. Travelin' can be hard on a body...and dangerous at times. The party I traveled with made it to Sacramento safe and sound, but others with the train didn't fare nearly as well." He pushed back the memory of a grave he helped dig.

"How so?" Her intense gaze telegraphed her interest.

"Half-way there, two families came down with

Cholera. The wagon master had to leave them behind or risk infectin' everyone." Billy took a deep breath. "Their pleadin' voices haunted me for a long time."

"You just left the sick folks alone to fend for themselves?" Disbelief clouded her wide eyes.

"It wasn't my choice, but I understand Mister McCullough's decision. Those who fell ill weren't his sole responsibility."

"Did you ever find out what happened to them?"

"No. I suppose anyone who died got buried on the spot, like those who journeyed before them. The Oregon trail is peppered with handmade crosses all along the way."

She shuddered. "Did you see anyone die?"

The memory brought a lump to Billy's throat. He swallowed hard. "One little boy."

"What happened?

"He fell out the back of his family's wagon and was trampled by the team followin' them."

She took in a sharp breath. "I don't want to hear anymore bad things. Tell me something exciting about the trip."

Billy cupped his chin. "Hmm, well, when the weather is nice and the travelin' easy, you see some beautiful country. On nights when spirits are high, you can expect music playin', dancin', and even a sing-a-long now and then."

Hattie covered a yawn. "With that pleasant image in my head, I'm gonna say goodnight. I'm tuckered out, and if Mister Franklin intends to leave at dawn, we'll have to start working in the wee hours to load the last minute things." She slid to the ground and cast a shy smile. "Good night, Billy, and thank you for sharing with me."

"It's the least I could do for someone willin' to bring me dinner. See you in the mornin'."

His gaze followed her until she disappeared inside. There was something about the glimmer in her eyes that made his heart beat faster. By some, she might be considered a child, but not by him. Those bow-shaped lips of hers just begged to be kissed.

Still hungry, he unwrapped the chicken and finished the second piece. He couldn't stop thinking about Hattie and how much he enjoyed the short time they'd spent together. He'd been on his own for several years—since Ma and Pa died from the fever. An only child, he wandered the country, taking odd jobs to pay for food and shelter. When Mr. Franklin approached him, Billy had jumped at the chance to be part of a family, if only for the time it took them to get to California. Six months with Hattie—maybe more depending on the weather. His pulsed raced at the thought.

* * *

Hattie returned to the house and found it dark except for a sliver of light coming from beneath the kitchen door. The soft clatter of dishes indicated the maid was still at work. After feeling her way upstairs, Hattie slipped into her bedroom. The wick she'd lit earlier had nearly burned to the end and flickered a warning. She blew out the flame and crossed to the window. Standing in the darkness, she peered out at the moonlit wagon that would be her home for the coming months. Knowing Billy Monroe would escort the family, made her feel safe. Warmth gathered in her chest and slid down her arms.

The silhouette of his movement played on the wagon bonnet but disappeared when he extinguished the light inside. Maybe on the journey, she might become better acquainted with him and find out more about his personal life. This strange attraction to him muddled her thoughts.

Hattie opened her mouth in a wide yawn. All the work she'd done during the day finally caught up with her. She shed everything but her undergarments and climbed into bed. Without the feather bed, her mattress lacked the comfort of the previous night. Billy was sleeping on one in the wagon, and she hoped it was hers. He smelled so…so manly—wood smoke, lye soap and leather.

Her soft chuckle rippled through the silence. What did she know of manly? Even more, why did Billy stir such unusual thoughts?

* * *

"Rise and shine, Miss Hattie." Though the room was dark, she recognized Tilly's drawl. "Best haul yerself outta bed and get movin'."

Morning already? Hattie moaned at having her sweet dream interrupted. Hadn't she just gone to sleep? Besides, Billy Monroe had been about to bestow her first kiss. Tarnation! She'd never experienced lip-on-lip contact, only a smack on the cheek, and that didn't count in romance. She sat up and heaved a sleepy sigh. "I'll be right down."

Tilly paused with one hand on the knob. "The mister

and missus are already up and having breakfast, best hurry if you wanna join them."

The nanny closed the door. Her footsteps faded as she walked away, but the aroma of fresh coffee lingered, making Hattie's stomach rumble. Before coming to the Franklins' she'd never been allowed to try it. Black tasted terrible, but milk and sugar turned the brew into a treat.

She hauled herself out of bed, lit the lamp and poured water into the basin. Shivering in the morning air, she washed her face, neck, arms, and hands. How did one bathe on the trail? In rivers and streams? No doubt she was about to find out.

After dressing, she ran her comb through her hair, secured her locks with a white ribbon, then spread up her bed. No use leaving a bad impression for the new homeowners. They must have paid dearly for the house, furniture, most of the linens and a lot of decorative items.

Poor Abby would have to start over again once they reached California. Of all the things she so wanted to take, the rocking chair where she sat and nursed the twins ranked highest on her list. Mister Franklin wouldn't even allow her one request. His actions reminded Hattie of bigger children who tried to run roughshod over the younger ones.

Despite Abby's contention that her husband really was a nice man, Hattie had yet to see actions that proved it. Her plan to steer clear of him was about to become a lot harder in the confines of a wagon.

She gathered everything in her valise, blew out the flame, then took one last look around the room. Fingers of dawn crept through the open curtains and provided light enough to see. At least for a few nights she had lived in a real home. With luggage in hand, she closed the door and made her way downstairs.

* * *

Exhaustion enveloped Hattie as she descended the stairs for the last time. She carried one sleeping twin while Abby followed with the other. Sniffling, Tilly stood near the front door, holding Zachary's hand. The whites of her eyes, normally a stark contrast to her dark skin, were bloodshot from crying.

Mister Franklin appeared from the parlor, checking his pocket watch as he had many times throughout the morning. He fell into step next to his wife. "Everything is loaded and ready. I've made a last check of the house to make sure."

At the door, he herded them outside. A pink and orange sky announced the sunrise.

"Well, I swear!" Frozen in place, Tilly jerked her gaze around to Abby.

"Oh...Elijah." Abby's voice crackled. The white rocking chair Abby so cherished hung from the wagon's side, secured with rope.

"Now, now, no times for tears. We've had enough of those." Mister Franklin took Eliza from his wife and handed the baby to Tilly. His hands circled Abby's waist, and he boosted her off the ground. "Step on the wagon wheel, then into the driver's box," he instructed. "You'll ride up front with me for the time being."

Tilly, sniffling louder, hoisted the little one up to her mother's waiting arms.

Standing next to her, Hattie was moved to tears. "Please don't cry. I promise I'll write you and let you know when we arrive safely."

"B-But, I cain't read." The colored woman dipped her chin to her chest.

"That's all right. I'm sure someone in the new family you'll work for can read the letter to you." She handed little Edwin to his father and enveloped the nanny in a hug. "I'll miss you," she whispered against ebony skin.

"All right. Enough goodbyes. If we don't get moving, we'll never make it to Independence on time." Mister Franklin handed the baby back to Hattie and scanned the street. "Where in Hades is Billy Monroe? He disappeared after he hitched up the oxen."

As if he heard his name, Billy trotted his horse up to the wagon, leading a cow with a length of rope. Damp hair clung to the nape of his neck and left watermarks on the collar of his sky-blue shirt. "Sorry, boss. I went for a quick dip at the bath house before I picked up ol' Bessie, here."

Hattie envied him—shining like a brand new penny. Sure, she'd washed up this morning, but visions of the claw-footed tub still haunted her. It probably wouldn't take long till she wished for her washbowl and pitcher over the cold water in lakes and streams on the way to California. Perhaps one day, she'd have a tub of her own. No one told her she couldn't dream.

"Get down and help me," Mister Franklin barked at Billy while boosting Zachary over the tailgate. "I expect you to earn what I'm paying you. Make sure the harnesses are secured as well as the water barrels."

Standing behind her employer, Hattie rolled her

eyes. The man acted like a horse with a burr under its saddle. Although she wanted to tell him to calm down, she dared not say anything. Keeping her head low, she waited for instructions.

Billy slid from his mount, secured the cow to the back of the wagon, and scurried up front. Bessie turned wide eyes to Hattie and mooed. The animal's udder hung like a turkey waddle, showing someone had recently milked her.

Mr. Franklin cast a stony gaze at Hattie. "Well, don't just stand there. Get in."

Eyeing the closed tailgate and wondering how to climb over, Hattie handed baby Edwin over to Tilly. Billy appeared at Hattie's side. Bending before her, he laced his fingers together to provide a step up. She placed her booted foot in his palms, and he hoisted her into the wagon as if she weighed only a pound.

"Everything's secure, Boss." Billy remounted.

Tilly brushed a kiss against the baby's forehead and handed him up to Hattie who knelt inside the wagon. She placed little Edwin on the featherbed pallet where he sucked his thumb and seemed content. Turning again to the tailgate, she locked gazes with Tilly, but neither spoke. Tears glistened on the nanny's dark cheeks as she crossed empty arms over her chest. A lump formed in Hattie's throat, but she managed a warm smile.

The wagon dipped under Mister Franklin's weight and lurched forward at the crack of his whip. Hattie held on, kept her balance, and waved goodbye. Tilly raised her hand in return before walking back toward the house, her shoulders slumped. Hattie struggled against tears for a woman she'd just met and already missed.

Billy trotted his horse close to the side of the Conestoga. "Well, we've started our adventure. Don't you worry yourself, Miss Hattie. I'm going to take good care of you and the Franklins."

All the anticipation and excitement for the trip now turned to fear. Hattie swallowed hard. Far more peril existed along the Oregon Trail than she had admitted to herself. Now with the journey beginning, a myriad of dangers played out in her mind. Could Billy really take care of everyone if Indians attacked the wagon? As she'd been taught at the orphanage, trusting in God calmed one's soul, and if ever one needed calming, it was hers.

Edwin began crying. Hattie swiveled around and stared at the red-faced child, his legs thrashing in the air.

The stark reality that she was now responsible for the children slapped her upside the head with all the gentleness of an anvil. Oh, why couldn't Tilly have come along? Not to do the job, but to be there to answer questions and offer guidance. Hattie lifted the baby to her shoulder and patted his back. "Now, now little one. We've a long way to go and I'm afraid you're stuck with me."

Sure, she'd done a lot of caretaking at the orphanage, but there had always been someone with authority around. Suddenly, she'd become that responsible person, and her ability to do the job satisfactorily wasn't quite as clear as she hoped.

The swaying wagon lulled little Edwin to sleep. Hattie laid him in the upper corner of the featherbed pallet, hoping he wouldn't wake for a while. He'd been fussy even though he had a full stomach and dry bottom. She sat, cross-legged, next to Abby, who'd dipped under the sheltering canvas to nurse the twins. Eliza's turn, she suckled noisily, her eyes heavy with sleep.

On the driver's bench, Zachary sat next to his father, his little shoulders squared. A smaller version of Mr. Franklin's straw hat shaded his head and eyes from the sun. For so young, he acted much older than four.

Food barrels took up most of the room in the wagon and created a privacy shield between the pallet where Hattie and Zachary would sleep and a larger one to be shared by the Franklins and the twins. The addition of a shovel, an axe, valises, and a few boxes filled with household goods the missus had managed to bring made for a cramped ride. Billy had told Hattie the women and children walked alongside the wagon during most of his previous trip, but she didn't look forward to hiking to California. Yet viewing the crowded space, she recognized why spending time inside would soon grow old.

"Well, we're really on our way." Abby's smile appeared forced.

"So, two weeks just to get to Independence?"

"That's what Elijah says...if the weather stays clear and the oxen keep a steady pace."

The time span didn't sound unreasonable until you tacked six months on top of it. The mere thought of spending that long listening to the wheels creak and groan and being jarred by the rutted road stole some of the excitement about the adventure. Hattie sighed. "Why did Mr. Franklin pick such big lumbering animals instead of mules?"

"Funny you should mention that. I questioned Elijah on the very topic. He says oxen are stronger and more reliable." She placed Eliza across her lap and buttoned the bodice of her gown. "I suppose the stubborn streak in mules comes into play when travelers decide which team to use. Lord knows it certainly wouldn't do to have a driver and the animals share the same disposition." Covering her mouth didn't mute her giggle.

Hattie bit her lip to keep from laughing. In her mind's eye, Mr. Franklin had long ears, dug in his heels and brayed at any suggestion thrown his way. She hid her grin behind her hand and tucked her legs to the side giving Abby access to place Eliza on the featherbed with her sleeping brother.

Abby crawled back to her space and sat, moving with the swaying wagon. "I suppose we'll be stopping for lunch soon." She rubbed her stomach. "What should we serve?"

"How about keeping it simple until we stop for the night? Maybe a biscuit and some salt pork?"

Abby nodded. "Sounds fine. We'll eat just enough to tide us over until dinner."

"Do you have writing material?"

Hattie's strange question raised Abby's brow. "Yes… but—"

"I thought it might be smart to plan dinners for the next several days."

"What a wonderful idea." Abby reached behind to a small suitcase, opened it, and produced a pencil and a pad of paper. She touched the leaded tip to her tongue then wove the wooden stick through her fingers, staring straight ahead. "Hmmm, let's see. We have potatoes, ham, canned vegetables, a few fresh apples, eggs…which we should save for breakfasts, and lots of salted pork. I think we may have some canned peaches and pears, too."

Hattie eyed the wooden barrels around her. "Billy says we have cornmeal and flour for baking."

Abby heaved a loud sigh. "I haven't baked in so long, I'm not sure I remember how. The last time I recall making bread was before my mother passed."

"Oh, don't worry." Hattie flicked a limp wrist. "I helped out in the orphanage kitchen, and the cook taught me how to make bread, biscuits, and even pancakes."

"But how will we bake anything? We have no oven." Abby nibbled her bottom lip.

"Pan fried biscuits are the best. We don't need an

oven, just a good hardy campfire. I'll teach you."

"I'm so glad you're here." Abby reached across and patted Hattie's hand. "I fear I've been spoiled most of my life." She lowered her gaze. "After having servants for all these year…"

"We'll make a fine team. You'll see." The wagon stopped so abruptly, Hattie fell against the wooden side.

Mr. Franklin poked his face through the canvas opening. "What's for lunch?"

* * *

With the noontime fare over and the twins still sleeping, Hattie reclined on her featherbed. Moving with the wagon's rhythm, she thought of Billy Monroe and her stolen glances at him during lunch. Something about him drew her gaze and stole her appetite.

Mr. Franklin had halted the team beneath a large tree where the adults and Zachary shared a blanket spread over the coarse grass. She hadn't eaten her biscuit and bacon, and now her stomach rumbled. She'd have to suffer through until dinner. Why hadn't she wrapped her lunch and saved it instead of refusing it? The habit she'd practiced so long in the orphanage had gotten lost in Billy's smile.

Perhaps she'd grab an apple.

Listening to the wheel's droning, she relaxed and enjoyed the last bite of her succulent fruit before hefting the core over the tailgate. Her eyes grew heavy and she closed them. Before sleep totally claimed her, a volley of gunshots and loud yells brought her bolt upright. On her knees, Hattie scrambled to the tailgate, crouched, and peered outside. Two riders closed in on the wagon, their horses churning up a dust cloud behind them. Guns drawn amid their whooping and hollering, they fired rounds skyward. The cow's eyes widened with each shot. The animal stretched her neck, attempting to break free of the rope binding her.

Billy rode back toward the two revelers, one hand on his pistol. The gunfire ceased leaving only the fearful thudding of Hattie's heart sounding in her ears. Mr. Franklin continued on instead of stopping. The crack of his whip sliced the silence, and the slant of the descending wagon obliterated any view of Billy. Worry niggled at Hattie. Two against one wasn't fair. Why didn't Mr. Franklin at least make an effort to help?

Hattie turned and cast a beseeching look at Abby, who sat up front with her husband and son. The woman's sideways glance along the ruffle of her bonnet and a shrug of her shoulders displayed her usual reluctance to confront her mister. Hattie considered screaming "stop," but swallowed her words. Her knuckles white from clutching the tailgate, she listened for the resuming sound of gunfire. She heard none.

The babies slept soundly, their slumber aided by motion. Hattie remained on her knees, her gaze searching the horizon. An unidentifiable dot bobbed to the top of the hill and grew in size until she recognized Billy's black hat and dapple-gray mare. A loud sigh fluttered Hattie's lips as she eased her grip and settled back on her heels. While relieved to see him, her curiosity piqued. She couldn't wait until he caught up with the wagon and shared what'd happened.

* * *

Billy flashed a grin as he galloped by. Her cheeks heated. She should have ducked out of sight instead of appearing to be a nosy Nellie. No denying she was one, she clenched her teeth and inched to the front opening in the canvas.

"Whoa," Mr. Franklin's slanting tug on the reins and bellow at the team stopped the turning wheels and sent her sprawling. She barely missed hitting her head on the wagon bench.

"Just a couple of drunks letting off some steam," Billy reported. "They've veered off the trail, headed for a ranch up north where they plan to join a cattle drive."

Hattie took a deep breath, pulled herself up and smoothed her skirt. Billy was so brave to face two men...especially ones toting weapons. What if they'd killed him?

One of the twins whimpered. Concerned with her duties, Hattie shook the frightening notion of Billy from her head, inched across the wagon, and fetched the child. The little ones had slept much longer than she'd expected. Hattie tapped Abby on the shoulder. "Edwin's awake."

Abby straddled the wagon seat, stepped into the bed and then dragged her other leg over. She tugged at her noticeably damp bodice. "I figured it must be feeding time." Her smile wasn't genuine.

By now the other twin began to fuss. Hattie handed Edwin to his mother and retrieved his sister. Edwin's simpering turned to a hungry howl, and soon Eliza joined in, creating a raucous duet. Abby offered her breast to Edwin, silencing his protests and leaving Hattie to soothe Eliza.

None of Hattie's attempts pacified the baby girl.

"Have you ever nursed them both at the same time?" Hattie's frustration mounted as she attempted to be heard over the child's wailing.

"No, and I don't intend to try." Abby's response was terse and to the point. "I had a hard enough time feeding Zachary when he was a baby, and when I learned I had twins, I was mortified." She smoothed Edwin's silky hair. "I love my children, don't get me wrong, but I find no joy in this part of being a mother. I look forward to the day I can wean them."

Hattie swayed back and forth, finally silencing Eliza. "I can't say I blame you, but then I've never looked far enough ahead in my life to consider I might be a real mother someday."

"Don't you intend to marry?"

Hattie sighed. "I've acted the mama for so long at the orphanage, I never expected I would leave there."

"Do you want children?" Abby pressed.

Hattie shrugged. "I honestly don't know. Right now, my responsibility is to your little ones."

With Edwin's appetite satisfied for the moment, Abby exchanged him for his sister and put Eliza to the opposite breast. While the girl child nursed, Hattie changed Edwin's diaper and tossed the wet piece of linen into the crate with others. When they stopped for the night, she'd hang them out to dry. With luck, they'd camp next to a creek and she could wash the really dirty ones.

* * *

The wagon creaked into Independence. The trip had passed much faster than Hattie expected, and she'd finally mastered handling three children in a confined space. The sleeping infants remained on a constant schedule and allowed her time to entertain Zachary.

Earlier, he'd grown tired and bored, riding between his parents, and joined Hattie to listen to a story from a large book compiled by the brothers Grimm. Zach especially enjoyed the "Hansel and Gretel" tale and widened his eyes each time Hattie spoke in her scariest voice, acting as the wicked witch who threatened the young duo in the story. Abby had brought along other books, but Zach always clamored for the same tale. By now, Hattie recited most of the lines from memory.

The story over and excitement building at the prospect of civilization, Hattie and Zach knelt at the wagon's tailgate and peered out onto the dusty and rutted street. Much like St. Louis, the scenery looked the same. Wooden walkways ran the front length of an array of businesses, and hitching rails stood with tethered mounts waiting numbly in the sun.

On the left, a muddy river widened, accommodating various watercraft. White smoke spiraled into the humid air from a steamboat's tall cylinders as passengers boarded by way of a slanted plank. Where were they headed? Did the river flow all the way to California? The smell of dust churned up by the wagon wheels filled her nostrils and drove her back from the tailgate. She pulled Zachary with her, and the two crawled to the wagon's front and peered out between Abby and her husband.

"That's the Missouri River." Mr. Franklin's deep voice answered the question posed by Hattie's mind. "Before we join the wagon train, we'll stock up at the mercantile." He answered her second question before she had a chance to ask.

Was Mr. Franklin a mind reader? She chuckled, hoping he wasn't or he'd know exactly how she felt about him at times. She ruffled Zachary's hair and released a loud breath. "Thank goodness we're stopping for a spell. We'll be able to get out and stretch our legs."

* * *

Despite wanting to see what Independence offered, Hattie had no time for lollygagging. By the time Mr. Franklin and Billy located the man responsible for leading the wagon train, there was only time left to visit the local mercantile to add to the supply coffers. Now, nestled between other wagons in a line formed on the edge of town, Hattie worked alongside Abby, preparing dinner and planning to retire early. A passing horseback rider had relayed news that the train would depart promptly at dawn.

Zachary stood at the tailgate, playing with his carved wooden toys, while Eliza and Edwin sat snuggly in their mother's rocking chair, secured by an apron tied around them. The flames from the campfire danced in their wide eyes as the twins watched the commotion around them. Hattie smiled. "Abby, look at your children. I wish they could talk so they could tell us what they're thinking at the moment."

Abby straightened and rubbed the small of her back. Her eyes narrowed. "I can tell you what I think." Her expression softened at the sight of the babies. "They do look amazed, don't they?"

"And this is only the beginning." Hattie pulled out the cast-iron skillet from the side storage outside the wagon. Toting the heavy utensil the short distance to the fire with one hand, she toted a bowl of dough tucked in the bend of her other arm.

* * *

Billy stood in the shadows between the Franklin wagon and the one in front and watched Hattie. Her hem skimmed the tall grass alongside the trail and the moonlight shone in her hair. The fixed set of her jaw showed determination as she knelt next to the fire and spooned dough into a crackling pan. When he'd first met her, she'd acted shy and retiring, but since leaving St. Louis, he viewed her in a much more mature light. Determination fueled his curiosity and desire to get to know Miss Hattie Carlson better...much, much better. He left the safety of his hiding place and approached the campfire. "Hattie." He drew her attention. "Would you like to take a walk?"

CHAPTER SIX

Dinner over, the dishes done and everything packed away, Hattie strolled along the endless ribbon of various conveyances with Billy. A full moon lit the darkened trail, while campfires burned brightly on the other side of the wagons where families and friends gathered. Mixed aromas from a myriad of dinners hung in the humid air, and somewhere in the distance, a jolly tune danced across the prairie as someone played a fiddle. Childish giggles and booming laughter sounded across the camps, displaying the joyful prospect of new beginnings.

Being careful to watch where she walked, Hattie glanced up at Billy. "Did you enjoy the meal?"

He patted his stomach. "Yes, ma'am. I truly did. Your biscuits were delicious, the coffee just strong enough, and the pork perfect."

"I'm glad my dinner met with your approval."

"Did your momma teach you to cook?" He kicked a pebble and sent it flying down the trail.

"No, didn't have a mother that I know of. I learned

at the orphanage."

He flashed a puzzled look. "Orphanage?"

"Oh, I guess you didn't hear. I grew up there. Cooking was only one of my many chores."

His loud sigh rent the silence. "I suppose you could consider me an orphan, too, since Ma and Pa passed away, and I don't have any other relatives."

"I'm sorry, Billy." She spoke past the lump in her throat. "I know what it's like to miss having family."

He shrugged. "I'm doin' fine. Reckon I've been too busy to notice the loneliness. Movin' from place to place, makin' a livin, by doin' this and that has kept me busy—not given me time to dwell on things."

Her frown turned to a smile. "What do you plan to do when we reach California?"

"I can't say I rightly know. I guess I'll have to wait and see what opportunities I stumble on. Until right now, I hadn't even givin' thought to stayin'." He clasped his hands behind his back. "Are you planning to keep workin' with the Franklins once we get there, or do you plan to get a different job?"

"Hmm, I 'spect I might stay on with the Franklins as long as they'll have me. I don't much care for the mister, but

Abby and I have become good friends in a short time. I really like her."

Billy chuckled. "Yeah, Mr. Franklin definitely isn't the kind you can cozy up to but I reckon there must be something good in him if he convinced Miss Abigail to marry him."

Hattie gave Billy a playful jab with her elbow. "Wonder what it is."

* * *

Standing next to Billy, Hattie gazed over the wide expanse of the Missouri River below. Muddied and hazed earlier, now the moonlight sparkled in the fast moving current and tinted the water blue. A breeze rippled through the tall grass at her feet. She shuddered at the chill. With their shoulders only inches apart, pleasant heat radiated from him. Her mind blurred with thoughts of Billy putting his arm around her and pulling her close so she could gain warmth from his body. Were these thoughts normal? She had no idea; they were all new to her.

Her pleasant reverie ended with a gasp. "Oh, Billy. How long have we been gone? I have to get back and help Abby get the children ready for bed. This was supposed to be a short walk."

Billy grabbed her hand. "It's my fault for keeping you out too long. I'll take the blame, don't worry."

His work-roughened palm against her smooth one sent chills of a different nature shivering through her. She struggled to keep up with his fast pace back toward the Franklin's wagon, but in all honesty, she wasn't in any hurry for the night to end. Billy Monroe was holding her hand, and she liked it.

* * *

"I'm so sorry." After the half-run back to the wagon, Hattie breathlessly blew out the words. She took a minute for her pulse to slow. "I hadn't realized Billy and I walked so far."

Abby hefted Zachary over the tailgate then cast a knowing smile at Hattie. "The twins are already sleeping, and I'm glad you enjoyed your stroll with Mr. Monroe. You like him, don't you?"

Hattie's cheeks warmed. "W-well, I-I barely know him…but yes, he's very nice." She dipped her chin. "Still, that's no excuse for shucking my duties. Please go enjoy the fire with Mr. Franklin. I'll change Zachary into his nightshirt and tell him a short story." She turned her attention to the lad in time to see his mouth open in a huge yawn. Holding her index finger across her lips, she smiled. "I promise we won't wake the babies."

Abby nodded. "Thank you, dear. I think I will join Elijah and spend a little time relaxing in my rocking chair before I bed down for the night. She pulled Zach's head toward her and, standing on tiptoes, kissed him on the forehead. "Goodnight, sweet pea. See you in the morning."

Hattie hefted herself over the tailgate, careful not to catch her dress on a piece of splintering wood cleaved from the last flour barrel hoisted into the wagon. She led Zach to the pallet they shared, changed him into his nightclothes, covered him with a light blanket, and then sat on her heels. "What story would you like to hear?" The beginning to Hansel and Gretel already formed on her tongue before the child even answered.

She hadn't relayed much of the fairy tale before soft snores told her Zachary slept. On her knees, Hattie shimmied out of her dress and dropped her nightgown over her head. Dawn wasn't that far away, and tomorrow promised to be a long and exciting day. She snuggled down next to her charge. The light smell of smoke drifted inside the wagon, and songs in the distance lulled her to sleep.

* * *

Breakfast finished, everything stowed back in its place, the wagon was ready to move. Mr. Franklin sat in his usual stoic manner, both hands holding the reins. Hattie peered between husband and wife, awaiting the signal to head west. The twins, wide awake, had already nursed, and now lay on their pallet. Edwin played with his toes and his sister watched him with wide eyes. Zachary, his straw hat low over his eyes, crouched in the far corner of the wagon bed with his small wooden horse and rider. The youngster's serious brow resembled his father's more each day.

Hattie craned her head farther out and glanced to Mr. Franklin's left. Billy sat astride his horse within arm's reach of the wagon, looking fresh and clean. She imagined he smelled of the soap, leather and musk that created his own personal aroma. Why these silly thoughts invaded her head, she had no idea. Whenever he was near, she lost all good sense.

"Wagons ho," came the command down the line...each driver yelling the words to the one behind.

With a snap of the reins, the Franklin's wagon

lurched forward. Hattie's nails dug into the wagon seat to keep her balance. Her heart hammered. This was it. The two weeks from St. Louis had been a mere rehearsal for the real trip, and now there was no turning back.

Abby glanced over her shoulder and clasped one of her hands atop Hattie's. "Well, we're truly on our way. I said a prayer last night for our safety, and asked God to guide us to and bless our new home."

"So did I," admitted Hattie.

Retying her bonnet bow under her chin, Abby smiled. "I feel much better after having met some of the folks traveling with us. After you went to sleep last night, Elijah and I took a walk. There's a doctor five wagons up from us, a judge a few more toward the front, and even a preacher."

"Seems we have everything but a lawman." Hattie chuckled.

Abby flashed a serious look. "No need to worry 'bout that. The wagon master is an ex sheriff, so we have our own little town on wheels."

Hattie's mind wandered. She'd lived in St. Louis all her life, but never felt like part of the town...not even welcome at times. During pleasant weather, the headmaster sometimes trooped the children down to the river for a picnic. Passersby cut a wide swath around the group, acting as though the waifs were unclean or carried an infectious disease. People who came to the orphanage were seeking young children to fill the gap in their family. Rarely, did someone adopt a child who had already developed a personality or grown taller than two feet. After being with the Franklins for only a short time, Hattie already had a sense of belonging, thanks to Abby. Maybe this trip to California was just what Hattie needed to realize her worth. If Billy valued her, that made things look even more promising.

Promising? The thought reminded her of a vow she'd made to herself long ago. If and when the time came for marriage and family, she aimed to adopt at least one older child. She knew firsthand how much it hurt to be overlooked time and time again when a family was all she ever wanted. Hattie remained determined to save at least one orphan from that pain.

"Where did you go?" Abby snapped her fingers in front of Hattie's face.

"Oh, sorry. I guess my mind drifted for a few minutes."

"I kept talking, but you were so lost in thought, you didn't hear a word I said, did you?"

"I heard most."

"Whatever it was you were thinking must have been pleasant because you had the widest smile on your face."

Hattie's face warmed. She dipped her chin and pressed a knuckle to her lips. Mr. Franklin didn't need to hear about her daydreams.

"Dare I guess you were thinking about Billy?" Abby pressed.

"Abby!" Hattie wrinkled her brow. "Unless you have a penny for my thoughts, I'm keeping them to myself." She ducked back inside the wagon to see to the twins.

* * *

Hattie slogged through the ankle-high grass with Abby at her side. Although the summer sun beat down with relentless heat, the cooling northerly breeze granted a respite not found within the confines of the wagon. The twins, clad only in their diapers, napped inside, while Zachary rode next to his father on the wagon seat. Powdery dust spiraled up from the wheels ahead and colored the air beige.

Abby sighed and whisked the back of her hand across her brow. "I feel like I'm wearing half the prairie on my face and between my teeth."

Hattie laughed. "I know. If it rained right now, we'd turn into a river of mud."

"I feel like we've walked for hours."

"We've barely walked at all." Hattie shielded her eyes and glanced up. "It isn't even midday yet."

"Great!" Annoyance tinged Abby's voice. "When I agreed to this trip, I didn't plan on walking all the way to California."

"Why don't you get back on the wagon? I'll walk until the twins wake."

"Look at all the other women up ahead." Abby gestured forward then looked over her shoulder. "And even more behind us. Elijah will think me weak if I insist on riding."

"I wonder how he would like to walk?" The words tumbled out before Hattie thought.

Abby's brow furrowed. "Hattie, that's not very kind. I have no idea how to drive the team, nor would I want to..."

"I'm sorry, Abby. I-I didn't mean to be sassy. It's just

that it wasn't all that long ago that you gave birth to not one, but two babies. That should allow you to ride more often than walk, don't you think?"

"You didn't do anything wrong." Abby's tone showed remorse. "I think I'm just overly tired and hot."

Hattie patted Abby's arm. "I'm sure we'll stop for lunch soon. Perhaps you can freshen up a bit before the twins awaken."

As if her spoken words declared a demand, the call of "wagons halt" came down the line. The two women exchanged an amused glance. "See, I told you," Hattie said. "I guess we had both better wash up and get lunch ready. The men folk will be starving." She glanced around. "I wonder where Billy Monroe is."

Gunshots sounded in the distance. Hattie grabbed Abby's hand, her eyes wide. "You don't suppose it's Indians, do you?"

More worried about Billy than herself, Hattie continued to scan the horizon for a glimpse of him.

CHAPTER SEVEN

Billy appeared in a cloud of dust, one hand yanking on the reins and the other dangling a prairie hen in the air. His horse skidded to a halt. "I've got tonight's dinner," he boasted, unaware that the additional veil of grit settling over Hattie stirred her ire.

"Was that you shooting off that dang rifle of yours?" Her hands rested on her hips.

He nodded, apprehension on his face. "I was—"

"Scare a body to death, why don't you." Tilting her head, she cast an icy glare at him. "I thought for sure we were about to lose our scalps." He didn't need to know she'd been frantic over his safety.

"B-but..."

"I don't have time for your excuses, Billy Monroe. I have to help Miss Abby here get lunch ready."

Abby stepped forward and reached for the bird. "Thank you, Billy. You've brought us a fine, plump hen for our dinner. Hattie, it seems has caught my grumpiness." She gave Hattie a sideways glance. "I'm sure we'll all feel better once the sun sets and the air cools down a bit."

Hattie rolled her eyes, her anger at Billy surging. "Humph, is he gonna pluck and dress our dinner, too?"

"Now Hattie. Let's not be rude." She cupped Hattie's elbow and directed her toward the wagon. "I'll bet the twins are awake and ready to eat."

* * *

Hattie gave Edwin's cherub cheek a playful pinch as she changed his diaper. His sister, resting next to him and dry now, cooed and pumped her chubby legs in the air. Free from the wagon's rocking and bumping, Hattie enjoyed the calm. Suddenly, from outside, an echoing scream raised the hair on Hattie's arms to stiff attention and brought her to her feet.

Leaving Edwin unswaddled, Hattie bolted to the tailgate and peered out, her heart in her throat. "Who was that?"

Abby, her hand to her bosom and eyes wide, glanced up. "I have no idea. The sound came from several wagons behind us."

"I'm gonna check it out." Billy scrambled to his feet, left his tin plate and half eaten ham slice in the grass, and hurried away.

Mr. Franklin shrugged and patted his wife's hand. "I'd best stay here with you and the children."

Of course, Hattie thought. Let Billy be the one to be brave while you stay here and act the part. The man was clearly a coward.

A fretful protest pulled her attention back to the babies. She returned to Edwin, secured his flannel and stood him up. "There, little man. Now you can go join Momma."

The scream still rang in her head. Only something dreadful could cause such a horrible response.

* * *

"Where's Billy?" Hattie's nosiness piqued.

She smoothed Eliza's curly locks off her forehead and jiggled her, wishing Edwin would finish nursing so she could hand over the hungry and fussing infant in her arms. If only she could wander down the line and learn what took place. Billy was taking forever.

Finally, she switched children with Abby, and having just climbed down from the wagon bed after placing a sleeping and content Edwin on his pallet, Hattie turned to find Billy approaching the camp.

"What happened?" She widened her eyes and held back the barrage of questions she had ready. She was still irritated with him from earlier, but her need to know about the scream outweighed her annoyance.

Billy's forehead beaded with sweat and his breathing rapid, he swept a serious gaze around the circle. "The Miller family found their daughter dead next to the stream."

Hattie gasped. "Dead? From what? How?"

Mr. Franklin leapt to his feet, his brow furrowed and his jaw tense. Abby straightened in her chair, her mouth agape, but still accommodated her nursing daughter beneath a modesty blanket.

Billy shook his head. "Looks like someone stabbed her. I probably shouldn't have poked my nose in, but I went to see for myself. Wasn't a pretty sight...I almost wish I hadn't looked. I'm sure her blank stare will haunt me tonight."

"Do they know how it happened?" Disbelief and fear lumped in Hattie's throat.

"Not as far as I heard." Billy sagged next to his plate and combed his fingers through his hair. "She went to get fresh water for coffee and when she didn't return, her ma went looking for her. That was her who screamed."

Abby removed the blanket from her shoulder and pulled Eliza from beneath it. She put the dozing baby to her shoulder and patted her back. "Oh dear, I'll have to pay Mrs. Miller a condolence visit, the poor woman." She looked to her husband. "What do you suppose happened, Elijah? Who could do such a horrible thing?"

He rubbed his chin and took a deep breath. "I have no idea, my dear." He turned his stern stare on Billy. "You and I need to make sure we keep a good eye on things around our wagon and never, never leave these women alone...at least until we know it's safe."

It wasn't long until word came that the wagons were moving again. Nothing more could be done for the Miller family, and any travel delay set the entire train in peril. Weather played an important part in whether or not everyone arrived in California before the snow started. Hattie climbed inside and took Eliza from her mother. Someone died but life went on for everyone else. Hattie dabbed a tear from her eye and considered how Mrs. Miller must be feeling. Hattie had never had a family to lose...at least none she remembered. She could only compare the pain of having a cherished friend adopted from the orphanage, but although she sensed the loss deeply at times, those occasions were more a cause for celebration.

* * *

The train stopped next to the Missouri River for the night, the wagons circled for protection. Kneeling at the riverbank in the fading sunlight, washing dirty diapers and a few of her own undergarments, Hattie heard music coming from across the camp.

Like sparks from a fire, lightning bugs rose from the thick prairie grass and put on a wondrous show of color. The dinner Billy had shot earlier now filled Hattie's belly and her mood toward him had improved dramatically. A half moon crept from the horizon, exchanging places with a weary sun. Hattie hurried to finish and get back to the wagon. Her nerves were on edge, and had the children not needed fresh swaddling, she wouldn't have ventured from camp. Billy stood uphill, his rifle in check, awaiting her return. An occasional glance back at him calmed her fearful heart.

Word had spread that tomorrow before the wagons moved onward, a short church service and funeral would be held for anyone interested. Hattie loved hymns, having learned them in the orphanage, and recognized the distinctive tune of Amazing Grace being rehearsed for Sunday morning. She hummed along while she wrung water from the cotton squares, trying to soothe her jangled nerves. She hadn't known the Miller girl at all, but Billy's declaration that she'd been killed next to water sent a quiver down Hattie's spine. She jerked around to the sound of approaching footsteps.

"You almost done here?" Billy stood over her, a piece of straw dangling from his full lips. "It's gonna be dark soon, and we should stick close to the wagon."

She hadn't even heard his approach and imagined how the Miller girl's assailant had sneaked up on her. Hattie's shoulder's tensed, but relaxed with the realization she had her own armed guard. Viewing the jaunty set of Billy's hat and the stray curl that hung on his forehead made her heart skip a beat. She took a moment to compose then smiled at him. "I'm on the last flannel. Thanks for looking after me." After gathering the wet pieces into a basket at her side, she dried her hands on her apron then stood. She tilted her chin and peered up at him. "I owe you an apology."

"Fer what?" He dragged the straw from his mouth,

his brow arched.

"This morning...when you came riding up with the prairie hen, I wasn't very nice."

"I was a little confused about why you were so dang mad at me."

She crinkled her nose, not wanting to admit the truth. Her gaze fixed on the ground.

"You were mad, admit it." Billy nudged her with his shoulder. "But tell me why. I still don't have a clue what I did that ruffled you so."

Her sigh sliced the lingering silence. "I wasn't mad as much as I was worried. When I heard the gunshots and didn't see you, I immediately thought the worse. I pictured some Indian brave waving your scalp with a bloodied hand."

Billy peered down his nose. "You ever seen an Injun?"

"No, but that doesn't mean I haven't heard stories."

He lifted his chin. "And just who told you such scary stories?"

"The headmaster at the orphanage." Hattie squared her shoulders. "He said people with red skin weren't to be trusted and had only killing white folks on their mind."

"That's not entirely true." Billy shook his head.

"White folks do just as much killing as Injuns."

An image of the Miller girl flashed through Hattie's mind, proof that Billy told the truth. She pushed the haunting face aside, hefted the laundry, and started back towards camp with the basket balanced on one hip. She cast a raised brow at Billy as she passed. "Well, if it's all the same to you, I'd just as soon not meet any Indians at all."

"Fine with me," Billy mumbled as he knelt near the water.

Pleased she'd apologized and smoothed any ruffled feathers, Hattie lifted her skirt with one hand and tramped through the knee-high grass. As much as she wanted to tarry longer and enjoy Billy's company, she had chores to attend. In the growing dusk, she spied three horsemen in the distance.

Swiveling back towards Billy who knelt, drinking from a cupped hand over the creek, Hattie pointed toward rising dust. "Riders comin'."

Billy rose and squinted in the direction she indicated. "Wonder who they are? He hurried to her side and took her elbow. "Let's get back to the wagons."

Her stomach flip-flopped as the heat from his touch traveled the length of her arm and into her chest. What about his nearness made her feel so strange? The sudden onset of emotion he stirred with a mere touch measured more concern than the approaching strangers, but taking large strides to match his, she kept pace, sensing his protective attitude and liking it.

In camp, Billy drifted off toward the front of the train, she supposed to investigate the new arrivals. She slipped between the Franklin wagon and that of the Smith family, ready to be scolded for being gone so long. Supper fires glowed all around camp, and mingled aromas hung heavy in the air. Abby stirred a huge pot suspended over leaping flames and smiled when she noticed Hattie. "Oh, there you are. I was starting to worry about you. Elijah wasn't happy that I let you go off to do laundry."

Zachary played on the ground near the rear wagon wheel, the twins watched with smiles and fascination etched on their angelic faces. Mr. Franklin sat like royalty in the rocking chair he almost refused to bring. Try as she might, Hattie just couldn't relate to the man.

Hattie placed the basket on the ground and began hanging wet laundry along the tailgate. "Billy was watching over me, but sorry I took so long." She wiped perspiration from her brow. "Whew, it's so warm tonight; these flannels will be dry in no time."

She directed her gaze to Mr. Franklin. "Did you notice the riders coming into camp?"

He craned his neck toward the lead wagon. "No. Do you know who they are?"

"I couldn't see them clearly, just plain enough to make out three men on horseback. Billy didn't recognize them either. I think he's gone to find out."

Billy, breathless again, strode back into camp. "Those three we saw are lawmen." He answered Hattie's question before she could ask it. "I heard the sheriff say they'll be asking lots of questions of folks on the train."

"Did someone send for them?" Abby looked at Billy and then to her husband.

"No," Billy answered. "They just happened to be lookin' for a couple of men who robbed a bank."

"Perfect timing, don't you think?" As always, Mr. Franklin's gruffness annoyed Hattie despite the situation calling for his attitude. It never seemed to change. Abby might insist he possessed a softer side, but Hattie had yet to see it.

"How can we help? We didn't see anything." Hattie set her basket inside the wagon. Her curious side looked forward to talking with the law but she couldn't admit that aloud. She moved to the sideboard, removed the coffee pot and began filling it with water from the barrel mounted on the wagon's side.

Abby stepped away from the fire, her hands clasped at her waist. "I try not to think about what happened, but the death of the Miller girl has me so frightened. How can we go about our daily routines when there might be someone dangerous amongst us?"

Her husband came, stood next to her and put his arm around her shoulders. "Don't fret, my dear. I'm here to protect you. Besides, it's quite possible that whoever did such a dastardly deed is long gone."

Abby peered up through misting eyes. "But why kill such a young woman? Men are usually the victims of such violence...ah, I know you understand what I mean, brawling, gunfights and the like."

He dabbed wetness from her cheeks with his handkerchief. "Of course. We do tend to be more involved in unsavory situations, but now that the law is involved, perhaps we'll get some answers. Between the two of us," he nodded towards Billy, "you have no need to worry." His glowering stare locked on Hattie. "And you, young lady, will not venture away from this wagon again without my say so. Understand?"

She stared down at the toes of her dusty shoes peeking from beneath her hem. "Yes, sir."

Looking up, she carried and placed the coffee pot over the flames then straightened. "I'm going to get the children ready for bed now, if no one has any objections." She fixed her gaze on Mr. Franklin. He, like the headmaster who rapped her knuckles many times, brought out her defiant side.

* * *

Outside, people bustled around their campsites, making breakfast and packing up to move on. The children were dressed and ready for the morning church service. The twins, already fed and content, played in the wagon and Zachary clamored to escape confinement. Hattie had just climbed out and held Zachary when the stranger sauntered into camp.

He rivaled Billy in every way: sun kissed skin, dark hair, broad shoulders, narrow waist...even the rugged good looks. Rather than sky blue eyes, sparkling chocolate ones peered from beneath the dust-powdered brim of his hat.

The daylight reflected from the gold star pinned to his shirt. Hattie slid Zachary off her hip and stood him on the ground. She smoothed her skirt with dampened palms and flashed a nervous grin. "H-hello."

The stranger doffed his Stetson. "Morning, ma'am. I'm Deputy Wainright, and I'd like to ask you a few questions if you aren't too busy with your little one." His eyes focused on Zachary.

Heavens, he couldn't think the child was hers. Words clumped in her throat. "O-oh, his mother is right over there." She pointed to where Abby stood with a group of women.

Zachary settled in the grass near the wagon and began playing with his wooden toys. Hattie, still wrangled by the nervousness elicited by her visitor, fetched a cup from the sideboard. "Would you care for coffee?"

"I'd appreciate that, Miss...or is it Missus?"

"Dear, where are my manners?" She extended her free hand. "I'm Miss Hattie Carson. I'm traveling as a companion to Mrs. Franklin to help with her three children.

He grasped her extended palm, sending a shock shivering up her arm. Was she so naïve and deprived of male attention that every young man would strike her stupidly giddy?

While fishing for something to fill the awkward silence, she used her skirt to lift the heated coffee pot then handed him a full cup. "I need to stay close to the wagon as the twins are inside, but..."She brushed by him and lowered the tailgate."Care to sit?"

Her mouth gaped when he set his cup on the sideboard, placed both hands around her waist and hefted her onto the wooden seat as if she weighed nothing. With coffee in hand, he sat next to her. He hung his hat on a wooden peg normally reserved for the washtub. She couldn't stop staring at the mass of waves tamped down by his head covering nor quell the desire to comb her fingers through them.

"I suppose you know we're looking into the killin' that occurred a few days ago?" His voice snapped her to attention.

"Y-yes, we were all stunned to hear about it."

"Did you know Miss Miller?"

Hattie shook her head. "Not really. We had only exchanged greetings in passing."

"Then you wouldn't know who she associated with or who might have been with her the day of her death."

"I'm afraid not."

He released a loud breath. "Seems the girl didn't socialize much. I'm getting the same response from everyone I question."

Hattie pointed to the twins, now awake and crawling about. "There isn't much time to make friends for some of us. I've met a few of the people in wagons close by when we stop for meals, but other than that..."

Billy rounded the wagon. His eyes widened beneath damp hair. "Oh, I-I see you have company."

"Have you two met?" Hattie slid to her feet, nervous for reasons she couldn't fathom.

"Not officially." Billy extended his hand. "Billy Monroe." He wore a clean shirt and pants, and his boots lacked the usual coat of dust.

The deputy stood and offered his palm. "Tom...Tom Wainright."

"Nice to meet you." Billy released from the handshake, retrieved a cup and poured his own coffee while glancing over his shoulder. "Havin' any luck finding out who killed the gal?"

"Sadly, no. I think this is one murder that might go unsolved, but we're going to keep trying to get answers before we leave."

"I hope that won't be soon...your leaving, I mean." Hattie's cheeks burned at such a bold admission. Billy's frown didn't go unnoticed.

Tom retrieved his hat and plopped it back in place. "No, ma'am. I'm sure we'll be here for a spell. Folks are a mite uneasy, and the wagon master requested we stay on as long as we can. Reckon' we'll just put off findin' the bank robbers for now."

He doffed the brim of his hat. "It was nice meeting you, Miss Hattie. I hope to see you again before I leave."

"I'd like that." Hattie's gaze braised the ground, her heart fluttered.

Her chin jerked up, and she stiffened when Billy stepped closer and put his arm around her. "We both appreciate the work you're doing, Deputy. Stop by camp whenever you can."

Billy removed his arm from around her and sidestepped away. He flashed a sheepish grin, wondering if she would say anything about his bold move. The redness in her cheeks and the manner in which she shifted from foot to foot showed her uneasiness without her muttering a word. He steeled himself and gathered his nerve.

"I thought he was payin' a little more attention to you than he should have. I wanted him to know that someone is lookin' out for you so he didn't get any notion that you're...."

"I'm what?" She stood with hands on her hips and used a demanding tone.

"W-well, I didn't want him thinking you were interested..."

"Interested in what?" She tilted her head and waited.

Billy stomped his foot. "If you'd let me finish a gol-darned sentence, I might be able to tell you what I mean."

Hattie released a pent-up breath. "Okay, I'm waiting."

She had the patience of a gnat. How could he tell her he had feelings for her when he'd only just realized them when he saw the gleam in the deputy's eyes? Sure, Billy had been taken with her since they'd met, but what seemed a casual friendship had blossomed into something more, but dang if he knew how to explain it.

"Fine." He huffed up his courage. "I got jealous. I didn't like the way he acted so comfortable with you." There, he'd said it. Admitting his feelings sort of left a bad taste in his mouth. He wasn't used to forming an attachment for anyone...hadn't for a long time.

The color drained from Hattie's face. Her throat wobbled with hard swallow. "Jealous? You were jealous of a stranger's attention?"

"He might have been a stranger, but he was sure wantin' to be more."

"How would you know that?" Hattie's brow arched.

"A man can read another man. Tom Wainright liked what he saw, and I know he'll be back."

Hattie cupped her arm through Billy's. "Well, if he comes calling, I'll make sure he knows I'm spoken for." She lifted her chin and peered up with a smile. "I am spoken for, aren't I?"

Boy, he'd put his foot in it now. By admitting his jealousy and showing he cared, he'd gotten himself into a relationship. Did he mind? Not really. She was special and he'd known that from the moment he laid eyes on her. Still he couldn't respond with the answer she obviously wanted. He grazed her cheek with a kiss and left.

CHAPTER EIGHT

Billy had given her a quick peck and walked away without any more discussion. She rubbed her cheek and puzzled over his strange reaction to Tom, and looking toward the wagon, she gasped. Edwin teetered on the edge of the tailgate, closely followed by his sister. Since they had learned to crawl, they were unstoppable, and now were beginning to try their luck at pulling up on anything close at hand.

Hattie sprang forward and stood in front of the two, guiding Eliza back the other way then snatching up her baby brother. "Eddy, Eddy, Eddy, you must be careful." She tweaked his cheek. "If you got hurt, your ma and pa would be very upset with me.

"Upset about what?" Abby rounded the wagon with Zachary in tow.

Hattie put Edwin back in the wagon and headed him towards the front before she closed the tailgate. "I keep forgetting they crawl now, and I was distracted by Deputy Wainright and then Billy. Edwin could have taken a tumble if

I hadn't noticed him."

"Hmmm, those are two distractions all right." Abby's interest focused on the young men instead of Hattie's negligence.

"You're quite right about that." Hattie blew a breath of relief. "Billy acted upset over the attention the deputy paid me, and I believe he considers we're sort of engaged."

"Engaged?" Abby's eyes widened. "Did he propose?"

Hattie gazed at the ground. "Well, he didn't actually ask me to marry him, but he…"

"Oh, Hattie, dear. Until he actually says the words and you set a date, you can do whatever you'd like. Now tell me more about this handsome deputy Wainright. I met him briefly at the Miller's wagon when I was paying my respects. He is quite a charmer, isn't he?"

A warming flush crept into Hattie's cheeks. "I should get back to the twins. I'm sure they both need changing, and it's almost time for services for the Miller girl."

"Yes, it's going to be a very sad start to the morning." She looked out toward the center of the circled wagons. "Oh, here comes Elijah to escort us. You crawl in and fetch the twins and I'll give Zachary's hands and face a quick wash. We'll talk about your handsome deputy later."

* * *

The funeral service had been heart wrenching. With no extra wood to build a casket, the body had been wrapped in a blanket and lowered into a shallow grave. The words spoken over the deceased were barely audible over Mrs. Miller's wailing, and in the wagon master's haste to get moving, the burial finalized with the laying of a few gathered stones being placed as a marker.

As the Franklin wagon rambled by a large oak, the grieving mother still knelt at her daughter's grave. Hattie's heart ached for her loss. Thoughts of being left beneath a mound of dirt made her shudder. Was there really a Heaven and Hell? So many questions went unanswered in her mind. As a child, she always wished for parents, now she prayed for a husband and children of her own. Would this trip be the answer to that prayer or, like the young Miller girl, her demise? A nervous twinge fluttered up her spine.

Hattie rode until the rocking wagon lulled the children to sleep, then slid over the tailgate to walk a while. The sun beat down with relentless heat, making her thankful for the wide-brimmed bonnet from Abby. An occasional breeze rifled the knee-high grass and brought momentary respite, but sweat adhered her gingham dress to her like cloying hands. How the children slept inside the stifling confines of the wagon puzzled her. At least, outside the air moved, and she enjoyed the break from caretaking.

A horse's snort blew moist air on her neck, and she jumped. She gazed up into the warm brown eyes of Tom Wainright.

He doffed his hat. "Good day, Miss Hattie."

At the deep timbre of his voice, goose bumps peppered her arms despite the growing heat.

"Good day, Deputy."

"It's a mite warm to be walkin', would you care for a ride?"

As inviting the thought of being cradled in his arms or sitting behind and hugging him might be, she was warm enough already. Besides, she probably didn't smell like a budding rose at the moment.

"No, thank you." She smiled up at him. "I enjoy walking. I don't get much time away from the children, so this is my opportunity to reflect."

"Oh...then I'm sorry to intrude."

She stumbled on a stone, but kept her balance. "N-no, you aren't intruding. I simply wanted to explain why I wasn't accepting your generous offer."

"Speaking of offers, I wonder if you might like to dine with me this evening. I'm not much of a cook, but I can whip up some bacon and eggs, and the fellas I'm travelin' with tell me I make a mean cup a joe."

Her heart hitched. She scanned the area for Billy. Would he be upset if he saw her talking to Tom? Probably, and that concerned her. She'd like to say something other than the deputy's rugged good look drew her attention, but she couldn't explain what did since she didn't really know him. His invite provided the perfect opportunity to remedy that and maybe figure out what about him created such a draw. But, Billy?

Abby's words echoed in her ears, reminding her Billy hadn't actually asked for her hand. Stood to reason she wasn't spoken for, so why did she feel so awkward? She squared her shoulders. Until Billy made clear his intentions, she'd do exactly what she wanted. If he asked about her decision to sup with Tom, she'd be happy to explain.

Concern over Billy's possible reaction got lost in a giddy haze. She peered up at Tom and nodded. "I'd love to join you."

Tom's grin broadened. "Good. What time would be best?"

"Now that presents a dilemma. The time we eat always depends on when the wagon master decides to halt for the night."

"In that case, I'll give you an hour to tend to the children before I come fetch you."

She swallowed hard. "I look forward to sampling your cooking." She hoped that would be all she'd sample. This courting thing was new to her, and she felt like a lost calf who'd strayed into a muddied hole.

* * *

Her hands locked around the warmth of her tin coffee cup and her stomach full, Hattie shared a log next to the fire with Tom. The separate stone ring he'd built away from where his traveling companions camped afforded some privacy. The light from the flames twinkled in his chocolate eyes and reflected in his badge.

Her thoughts drifted to the funeral, whoever killed the Miller girl, and how much danger was involved in finding the person responsible. Had the culprit left the train or did he still lurk nearby? No matter how she tried to tamp down her negative thoughts, they kept cropping up.

"So," his voice sliced into her thoughts. "Where did you grow up, an how did you come to be with the Franklins?"

She gulped. Did she really want to reveal her boring past? How much more exciting her tale would be if she had grown up on a fancy ranch with horses, cattle, and parents. "The story of my life is less than exciting." Maybe he'd decide to talk about something else.

"I know my job might fascinate people, but trust me, my childhood tales are pretty dull. Yours can't be any worse."

She dipped her chin. "I grew up in an orphanage in St. Louis. If I had parents or a different name, I don't even remember them." Her gaze lifted for his reaction as she sipped her coffee.

"Were you treated well?"

She lowered her cup. "Most of the time. There were some who weren't very nice, but mostly, the caretakers were so busy with other children, unless I did something to make myself stand out as a troublemaker, one day blended into another, and I grew up before I realized I had."

"How come no one ever adopted you?" His wide

eyes showed surprise. "O-oh, I'm sorry, that seems like a real personal question."

"It's all right. You can ask. Few people came around when I was younger. By the time I reached ten or eleven, so many little ones had come to the orphanage, I got lost in the crowd. Those seeking children want ones they can teach and grow to love, not ones already set in their way, like me." She chuckled. "I made it my job to love those who got left behind because I know how much it hurts." She held out her cup. "Can I have more? You do make good a good brew."

He poured her cup full and set the empty pot aside. "No wonder the Franklins picked you to tend their children. You've had lots of training."

She smiled, staring into the dark liquid. "I certainly have. Leaving the orphanage was the hardest decision I've had to make, but I realized I couldn't stay there forever. When I saw Mr. Franklin's ad at the Mercantile, this trip seemed the perfect way for me to build a life for myself."

She glanced up at him. "What about you? Where are you from?"

A strange sadness clouded his eyes. "Oh...here, there and everywhere. Like you, I don't have much memory of a family. My ma and pa died when I was around ten, I reckon. Even that's cloudy in my recollections."

She straightened. "Surely, you haven't been on your own since then?"

He chuckled. "No, a neighbor took me in and raised me...if you can call it that."

"What do you mean?"

"The old geezer lived by himself, and although I was scared to death, being alone and all, I thought he might be as hungry for family as me. Turns out he was more interested in finding a field hand, and I fit the bill."

She widened her eyes. "That must have been a terrible experience. Was he mean to you?"

"Not as long as I did my work and didn't sass, but I got my share of whoopins."

"I'm so sorry." She patted his hand. "I got my knuckles rapped more times than I care to remember by the headmaster of the orphanage school, but I never got beat."

Tom's chin dipped. "Mr. Radcliffe imbibed pretty regular. I swore I'd never drink if spirits make you as mean as he was most of the time."

Her heart ached for her new friend. "I vowed to never punish someone because they couldn't answer my questions." She chuckled. "I guess even though we didn't have the best growin' up times, we both learned something pretty important."

Tom's gaze turned to her. "That's why you got hit? Because you didn't know the answer to a school question?"

"Yes. If the headmaster had taken time to know me, he would've realized I didn't have much time for my lessons after class. Between chores and telling the younger ones stories to keep them entertained and out of trouble, I had pretty sore knuckles most of the time." She clasped her hands in memory, wringing and massaging away the old stings.

"Bet you wish you could meet him now, but while carrying a big stick." Tom grinned.

"Sure do, although I'd like to think I'm a better person than that. Besides, I wasn't the only one he picked on." She released a big breath. "Didn't you have any brothers or sisters?"

"None I recall. Like I said, I barely remember going to my folks' funeral or anything before then. I recollect bits and pieces from time to time, but my past is pretty hazy."

"Maybe it's for the best." She drained the last of her coffee and handed him her empty cup. "I suppose I'd best get back to the Franklin's wagon before everyone settles in for the night."

Hattie stood and smoothed her skirt. "Thank you for a delicious supper and good company. I enjoyed myself."

He rose. "I'm glad you came. I'm not sure how long we're going to be in camp, but I hope I get to see you again before I leave. If I'm still here, would you like to take a walk tomorrow evenin' after you put the children to bed?"

Billy's soulful blue eye flashed through her mind. She felt bad enough about supping with Tom without Billy knowing, so seeing him again on the sly just seemed dishonest. She flashed a half smile. "I probably shouldn't leave Miss Franklin to do the work I'm supposed to be doing. After all, I need to earn my passage to California." She'd told the truth, somewhat.

His smile faded. "I understand. Let me escort you back to your wagon." He grasped her elbow. "Remember, no straying off by yourself at any time."

Why did she feel so bad for turning him down? She lifted her skirt hem and watched where she walked, careful of the ruts and fallen twigs. "After what happened to the Miller girl, I'm not going anywhere by myself."

* * *

Hattie sat next to the campfire while Zachary ate his breakfast. She nursed a bitter cup of coffee and widened her eyes when Billy rounded the wagon.

"Good morning." He doffed his hat. "I came by last night to invite you for a walk but Mrs. Franklin said you'd gone to have supper with a friend. Did you have a good time?"

She stood, her knees wobbly. "I did, thank you."

"I didn't realize you'd made any new friends, what with being so busy with the children and all."

Hattie swallowed hard. "So I take it, Abby didn't mention who my friend was?"

"No, and I didn't ask. Should I have?"

Picking at her skirt, her stomach knotted, Hattie's gaze focused on a pebble just beyond her foot. "I may as well tell you since you're bound to find out sooner or later." She raised her chin. "Tom invited me to have supper with him, and I accepted."

The veins in Billy's neck bulged, and his face flushed. Hattie prepared for his anger to spill out. "We're just friends," she added, hoping to drown the fuse before the dynamite went off.

He took in a deep breath and exhaled. "Well, I'm glad you had a nice time. I 'spect Tom and his fellow lawmen won't be around much longer since no new leads have turned up to keep them here." He doffed his hat again, but his icy stare chilled her. "I hafta see to Bessie and hopefully scare up some game for dinner." He spun on his heel and left her with 'goodbye' dangling on her tongue.

She shook her head. Had she made a mistake by being with Tom? She hadn't done anything wrong, so why couldn't she swallow the lump of guilt gathering in her throat? If Billy was mad now, she hated to think how angry he'd be if she'd accepted Tom's offer for a walk. Billy didn't own her, and she was free to do as she pleased, so why had she turned Tom down? All the questions racing through her mind made her head hurt.

"Can I play now?" Zach tugged at her skirt.

"Oh, sweetheart, I totally forgot you were here." She knelt, grasped his shoulders and peered into his pure blue eyes. "You're such a good boy. Of course you can play. C'mon, let's go get your toys." She rose, took his hand and walked toward the wagon.

Life had become more complicated since leaving the orphanage. Billy set her stomach a flutter, but

Tom...something about him drew her to him like fish to a worm.

CHAPTER NINE

"Why didn't you tell me your new beau invited you to spend the evening with him again?" Billy slapped his hat against his pant leg, sending a flurry of dust into the air.

Feeling ambushed, Hattie's mouth gaped, but she finished changing Edwin's wet bottom on the tailgate, watching Billy from the corner of her eye. She hadn't noticed his approach, and now he stood by the wagon wheel, looking madder than a hornet someone swatted.

"Well, are you going to answer me or not?" He plopped his hat back on his head and crossed his arms over his chest.

Edwin's legs pumped the air in his eagerness for Hattie to finish. She placed the securing pin into his diaper, turned him over, and gave his rear a playful swat as he crawled toward his twin. She closed the tailgate and turned to Billy, her gaze matching his. "I've never reacted well to demands. Usually they were followed by punishment, so if you want my attention, I expect you to talk to me in a very different tone." She lifted her hem and brushed past him, plunging the dipper into the water barrel and taking a drink.

"Well, ah...y-you failed to mention Tom invited you to take a stroll with him tonight, and when he told me, I saw red."

"And why did you see red?" She tilted her head. Maybe taunting him would force him to state his intentions.

He cleared his throat. "I-I sort of thought you and me... ah, I supposed... Oh, dang it Hattie, you know what I mean."

"I'm not sure I do." She tapped her forefinger against her chin and looked at the sky, feigning deep thought.

"Well, if you can't figure it out, then never mind. Go ahead, have a nice time tonight." His jaw visibly tight, Billy spun on his heel and disappeared around the wagon.

Chuckling at Billy's frustration, Hattie glanced to the midday campfire, where Abby cleaned up lunch's remains. Mr. Franklin sat on a nearby crate, re-braiding the loose ends of a lead rope. Abby, the coffee pot in one hand and dirty cups in the other, crossed to the sideboard. "I couldn't help but overhear. Seems Mr. Monroe has his tail in a knot."

Mr. Franklin clucked his tongue against his teeth. "I'll leave you women to your wiles and see to the team. I'm sure the wagon master will want to get back on the trail in a few minutes." Using his forearm, he coiled the rope and left.

"Do you need help?" Hattie asked Abby.

"No, I'm just going to rinse out these cups and I'll be done. There wasn't much to do."

Hattie, her skirt lifted, and stepping lightly, crossed ankle-deep grass. She sat on the upturned crate the mister had vacated and stretched her arms over her head, arching her back at the same time. "Billy did seem upset, didn't he?" She giggled, smoothing her hands along her skirt. "Tom's just a friend. He invited me to take a walk tonight, but I turned him down. Besides, he'll be leaving anytime now, and I probably won't ever see him again." The thought of his departure carved a hollow feeling inside her. She stared into smoldering embers.

"The look on your face tells me that bothers you?"

Hattie's chin jerked up. "The thought of what?"

"Tom's leaving."

"Oh," she gave a dismissing wave. "Not really. I don't even know him that well." Hattie splayed her fingers through Zachary's hair as he played on a blanket next to where she sat.

"Perhaps you're bemoaning the fact that you won't have time to get to know him better."

Hattie sprang to her feet. "I have to see to the twins. They're being far too quiet." Not caring about the depth of the grass, she skirted through the sun-dried blades. She hated to see Tom go, but it wasn't for romantic reasons, of that she was sure.

* * *

Hattie awoke to raised voices outside the wagon. She propped herself on her hand and peered over the privacy wall to find the babies still sleeping, but their parent's gone. Next to her, Zachary's even breathing caused his blanket to rise and fall in a steady pattern as he slept despite the nearby ruckus.

Stepping softly as a cat on padded paws, Hattie slipped on her gingham dress, pulled on her socks and boots, and ran a brush through her sleep-tangled locks. With a ribbon securing her hair away from her face, she slipped over the tailgate and walked unseen to the gathering. Abby noticed her and came to stand beside her. Hooking her arm through Hattie's, the woman's misty eyes reflected a mixture of sorrow and fear.

"Mrs. Miller has killed herself." Abby blinked free the tear suspended from her long lashes.

"What? How do you know it wasn't the work of the person who killed her daughter?" Her mouth pasty and dry from sleep, Hattie's voice crackled with a deepness of someone just waking.

"Her husband witnessed her death." Abby held a fisted hand to her mouth and nipped at her knuckle. "He says she couldn't live with the belief their daughter, Anna, took her own life. Mrs. Miller hasn't been right since then, and constantly expressed a desire to join Anna."

"Her daughter killed herself, too?" Hattie widened her eyes. "Why?"

"Mr. Miller says Anna was never a normal child...that he and his wife had to keep a close watch on her to make sure she didn't harm herself or anyone else. They joined the train to find a new start away from people who knew her and made fun of her. Although she was nearing her sixteenth birthday, her father says she had the mind of someone much younger."

Hattie swallowed hard. "How did Mrs. Miller die?"

"She stabbed herself this morning before breakfast. She was cutting up some salt pork and turned the knife on herself."

"Oh, my Lord." Hattie glanced across the crowd at Mr. Miller. His red-rimmed eyes showed his sorrow and his pale pallor, his shock. She looked back to Abigail. "The poor man. He's been through so much sorrow. Should we offer to help prepare his wife for burial?"

The idea repulsed Hattie. She had no desire to see a dead person, but common decency compelled her to ask.

Abby patted Hattie's hand. "That's very sweet of you, but some of the other women are tending to Mrs. Miller. The pastor will speak at the grave before the train starts moving this morning. Would you please check on the twins and Zachary? We need to get them fed and dressed before the services.

* * *

Hattie had never heard a grown man sob, and her heart ached for Mr. Miller. He fell to his knees at his wife's grave and wept openly. She peered across the crowd at Tom, who stood with hat in hand next to his lawman friends. Was Mrs. Miller's loss the reason for the sadness displayed in his eyes or did Billy's arm around her speak louder than any words she could convey? She leaned into

Billy, taking comfort in his embrace, and hoping Tom realized she had room in her life for only one man—Billy. He was truly the man of her choosing, and Tom had been only a short-term distraction to the new world of courting. Still, she felt drawn to him.

Chapter Ten

The service ended and the crowd thinned. Hattie walked hand and hand with Billy back to the wagon, leading Zachary, and following the Franklins. Little Emily peeked over Abby's shoulder and flashed a grin, revealing her new tooth, while Edwin fidgeted in his father's awkward grasp. The sound of Mr. Miller's weeping sounded over the crackling of trampled grass.

"Load up!" The wagon master's call sliced the air. "Five minutes till we move out."

Again, distance and time didn't leave occasion for grieving and such. Poor Anna Miller had barely been cold in her grave before the wagons rolled westward. Now her mother lay beneath a mound of earth still wet from her husband's tears. Hattie's heart turned leaden as she accepted Billy's help into the wagon bed and took the children one at a time as they were handed over the tailgate to her.

The babies squirmed, babbling with an innocent happiness, unaffected by the silence and sadness. Zachary's confusion was lost the moment he grasped his toys and began galloping his wooden horse across a flour cask.

"Are you all right?" Billy peered up.

"Yes, I'm fine. Thank you for being...well, you know." Her cheeks warmed.

"He plopped his hat atop his head. " No problem." He gazed up as if he wanted to say something else, but instead touched the brim of his hat in a respectful gesture and smiled. "I best get up front and help get the animals hitched before Mr. Franklin comes looking for me."

Hattie forced a return smile. "Yes, you'd better. This day has already had a bad enough start to it, we don't want to tempt fate."

Billy disappeared around the wagon and Hattie sat, reflecting on the Millers' loss. Noticing Zachary's movement from the corner of her eye, she yanked on his pant leg. "You'd better sit down. We're fixin' to move."

The words had barely left her mouth when the sound of a whip lashed the air and the wagon jerked forward. The crawling babes teetered for a moment, then continued their curious inspection of everything they could touch or see. Hattie heaved a loud sigh. "Oh, having you two moving about has certainly made my days more tiring."

Her shoulder's sagged under the weight of her sadness, but she watched the twins with an eagle's eye.

"Miss Hattie?" Her reverie ended at the sound of Tom's voice. She glanced to the tailgate and saw his handsome face bobbing up and down outside the canvas. She almost laughed, but stepping carefully, she braced herself against the wagon's framework and inched her way to the back of the bed, where she knelt. "Hello, this is a pleasant surprise. What are you doing?"

He sat astride his roan, tall in the saddle; a fine figure of a man. Her heart fluttered for a moment, but only because such a handsome man paid attention to her.

"I came to say goodbye." He pulled back slightly on the reins to slow his horse and keep pace with the wagon.

"You're leaving?" A frown tugged at Hattie's lips.

"I'm afraid so. There's no need for us to stick around any longer since there was no crime committed. Sad about the momma and her daughter though."

"Yes, it certainly is a tragic loss, especially for Mr. Miller, and I understand you need to be on your way, but I'm truly sorry to see you go."

"Maybe if we'd met another place and time, things would have been different, but it appears you already have a beau...and might I add, he seems like a fine man." Those chocolate eyes that usually sparkled held no light.

Touched by his admission, she nodded. "Yes, Billy hasn't really made his intentions clear, but I do care a great deal for him." She stretched out her hand. "I wish you a safe trip Tom Wainright, and may God bless and keep you."

He grasped her fingers for just a moment then released them as though they burned him. He doffed his hat. "Same to you, Miss Hattie. Stay well and be happy."

He jerked the reins to the left and nudged his mount past the wagon. A combination of relief and sadness washed over her. She cared for Tom, but not nearly as much as she did for Billy Monroe.

* * *

Hattie knelt by the river, scrubbing soiled flannel clean on the stones along the bank. With two babies, keeping them in clean diapers was a constant chore, and as long as they camped near a river, stream or creek, the skin on Hattie's hands was doomed to remain puckered from being in the water for so long.

A week had passed since Tom and his friends left the train. Although there'd been no murder to solve, seeing

Mr. Miller traveling alone and so sad tugged at her heart. On the other hand, Billy's mood had improved. His jealousy no longer threatened, he reverted back to the happy-go-lucky fellow Hattie'd first met. Speaking his emotions might be difficult for him, but the shade of green he'd turned around Tom definitely let her know how much he cared for her.

Standing nearby, his rifle at the ready, Billy's gaze scanned the area. Earlier in the day, the train passed by the scant remains of a dozen or more buffalo that, according to the scouts, were slaughtered by the local Cherokee.

"You don't think the Indians are still around, do you?" Hattie glanced over her shoulder and cast wide eyes at Billie.

"Nah, they're probably long gone, but you can never be too careful." He draped his rifle strap over his shoulder, allowing the weapon to dangle, and walked closed. "You almost done?"

"Yes." She wrung the water from the last diaper and tossed it into the laundry basket. Standing, she massaged the small of her back. "How do you think the scouts knew Indians killed those buffalo?"

He bent and picked up the wicker container.

"Besides seeing arrows amidst the remains, the way the feathers are notched usually tell which tribe left 'em. If a white man had done the killin', they would have simply skinned the animal and left the rest. The Indians take pretty much everything. The meat, they use for food, the skins for blankets and coverings for their lodges. Bones serve as utensils for cookin' and eatin', and the some of the innards become bowstrings and thread for their sewin'. I hear tell they use the animal's bladders to tote water."

The unpleasant thought of water carried in that manner caused Hattie to make a face. She wanted to hear more, but Billy dropped the laundry basket at his feet and held a silencing finger to his lips. She cast a questioning look his way, but complied, freezing in place. He craned his ear toward the high grass to his left and pulled his rifle from his shoulder. Placing one foot steadily in front of the other, he approached the dense growth.

A cold chill ran down her spine, but her apprehensive gaze followed his movement. She strained to hear something, but Billy walked on silent feet, causing only the slightest crackle of grass as he parted the crispy strands. He disappeared from sight, leaving her quivering with fear.

Hattie waited, anxious to see him reappear,

counting the seconds as they ticked by. The tall reeds had gobbled him up, and the lump in her throat grew from fear that a swallow would make a noise.

"Swim for it!" The startling urgency in Billy's voice raised her hackles. "Hat—"

Something choked off the rest of her name.

CHAPTER ELEVEN

June, 2010 – Kearney, Nebraska

"Are you all right?" A deep voice above drew Hattie to lift her chin. She pushed back her bonnet and peered up as a stranger squatted next to her. He certainly wasn't an Indian and, for some strange reason, she didn't feel threatened. His broad smile, strong jaw, and coloring looked vaguely familiar.

"I think so." Rolling to her side, Hattie pushed herself into a sitting position and swiped streaming water from her face to better assess the man.

Dark spectacles hid his eyes. Light brown hair, cut short and impeccably combed framed a handsome face. He wore a shirt made from material strange to her.

"Let me help you up." Before she had a chance to object, he grasped both her hands and yanked her to her feet. She embraced herself to quell her shivers. Who was this man? He wore no hat, no boots, and britches in a fabric she didn't recognize. And what of the strange spectacles that hid his eyes?

He raised the dark glasses and allowed a sky-blue gaze to wander her soaking gown before he looked at her with an arched brow. "I stopped because I thought I heard someone screaming...oh, how uncouth of me. You're freezing." He pointed up the hill. "I believe I have a blanket in the trunk of my car, let me get it for you."

Car? She made a cursory inspection of him, noting the sharp crease in beige pants, a narrow belt with a thin silver buckle, and a strange little marking of some sort above a neatly sewn pocket on his pale blue shirt. She tapped the palm of her hand against the side of her head. Maybe she'd swallowed more water than she thought. Removing her drippy head covering, she wrung the water from it then secured it on her head again with the wet ribbon tied snuggly beneath her chin.

Her rescuer turned and fled up the grassy knoll, returning in seconds with a brightly striped blanket that he wrapped around her shoulders. "Better?"

"Y-yes, thank you." She pulled the ends tighter around her and basked in the warmth. Craning forward, she peered up river, hoping to see Billy. Was he okay? Her heart hammered with fear over what might have happened to him.

"How did you fall in?" The stranger's question pulled her attention away from the water.

She straightened and clutched the blanket with trembling fingers. "I didn't fall, I jumped because Billy told me to."

"And who is Billy?" Again the arched brow.

"He's traveling with the Franklin's, too, helping the mister with the animals and keeping watch. He was with me at the river while I washed the children's clothing. I just know something horrible has happened, and you have to help me find Billy and make sure he's all right." She grabbed the man's shirt front and peered up at him with urgency.

The stranger pried her fingers from his clothing, stepped back and held her at arm's length by clasping her trembling hands. "You aren't making a lot of sense at the moment. Traveling by wagon? Washing clothing in the river? Perhaps you should sit down."

She shrugged free of his grasp and straightened her shoulders. "I'm quite fine, thank you. It's Billy I'm worried about."

"You mentioned children...yours?"

She drew back and stared at him. "No, of course

not. I'm not yet married. I'm traveling with the Franklins purely to help Miss Abigail with her three youngsters until we get to California." She stepped toward the bank and leaned out, her gaze searching for Billy.

"I'm sorry if I offended you, but when you mentioned children, I assumed...."

She turned back to him and gulped down her fear. "No apology necessary, but I would beg of you to help me get back to the wagons. I know something has happened to my friend, and we must warn the others."

"And where exactly are these... these wagons?"

"Not far. I wasn't in the water very long, so I imagine if we follow the river back a ways, we'll come upon the train. First, we'll have to make sure it's safe to approach." She removed her blanket and handed it back while nodding her chin toward the other bank. "Of course, I'm on the wrong side, but I'll figure out how to get back across."

The stranger pointed down river. "There's a bridge not far away."

"Really?" Her relief released in a sigh. "Then can you please take me back? I have to make sure everyone is safe.

"Safe from what, Miss..." He stuck out his hand. "I'm

sorry, I should have introduced myself. I'm Case Atkins, and you're...?"

"Hattie Carson." She bobbed a quick curtsy. "I appreciate you coming to my rescue but we really don't have time for small talk. We need to move."

He grasped her skirt. "I suppose you're dry enough to ride in my car so I can take you back to your...your—"

She slapped the material from his hand. "Dry enough?" She raised her brow, curiosity gnawing at her. "And what is this car you speak of?"

"I have a Corvette...a red one...a convertible. I've only had it about a month, and I really don't want anything wet on my leather upholstery."

A million questions ran through her mind, but the panic and frustration knitting a nervous knot in her stomach overrode her need for answers. "Please, can't we just go? I have no idea what you're talking about...Corvette, upholstery, convertible. Other than the Franklin's wagon, I've only ridden once in a buckboard, but I'm sure whatever you're driving will be fine."

"Wagon and buckboard?" He burst into laughter, then calmed. "Are you part of a crew from a dude ranch or something...I mean you're certainly dressed the part."

Hattie stomped her foot, her ire heating her cheeks. "I don't appreciate your attitude. You must see the seriousness of my predicament. Something has certainly happened, and I can't be certain that by now even the Franklins and the rest of those traveling with the train are all right. We must hurry."

"Miss Carson, you aren't making any sense." The puzzled look in Case's eyes supported his words. "What kind of danger? Hurry and do what?"

She grabbed his arm. "I'm afraid Billy has been ambushed by Indians. If so, the people on the wagon train would surely be their next target."

Case drew back and studied her face. "Indians?" He gazed first to the left then to the right. "Is this a joke? Am I on television?"

She clawed at his sleeve. "Please, Mister, I don't have time to play word games with you. Think of the children and their safety."

He shrugged lose from her grasp. "I suppose the only way to make you relax is to drive you back to where these supposed wagons are."

"Oh, thank you." She released a loud breath. "Which way to your conveyance?"

"Conveyance?" He grumbled and pointed uphill. "I should have just kept driving."

She lifted her skirt hem and started climbing, but cast a side glance at him. "I heard that. I'm sorry you regret saving me, but right now my biggest concern is getting back to the wagon train."

"So you keep saying." He rolled his eyes.

Hattie lifted her skirt and started uphill. "I just hope we aren't too late because of the time we've wasted."

"I honestly meant no offense. It's just I've never met anyone quite like you before." Cupping her elbow, he helped her crest the incline.

At the top, Hattie skidded to a halt, her jaw gaping at what she saw.

"She's a beauty, isn't she?" Case stood with hands on his hips, his stance broad and his smile wider than the river. I can do zero to sixty in a blink of an eye."

Her gaze surveyed the shiny red object. "What exactly is this thing?"

"Surely, you're joking." He turned to her and with a hand on her shoulder, urged her closer, then used something silver and shiny to open what he called a door. "Get in please. I really think I should drive you to the nearest hospital. Clearly you're suffering from hypothermia or maybe a bad bump on the head."

She jerked away from his touch and sat, her mind spinning in confusion. "There is nothing wrong with my head, and I have no idea what other ailment you think plagues me. Please, just get me back to the wagons. You can explain this...this machine later."

Case closed her door crossed to the other side and got behind a huge wheel. He shut his door, and when he turned a key, a loud whirring sound sliced the silence. Hattie's shoulders tensed and she fisted her hands so tightly in her lap, her nails bit into her palms.

CHAPTER TWELVE

After explaining to Hattie the necessity for her seat belt, Case's frustration welled until his fumbling fingers could barely buckle his own. Stomping on the accelerator, he sent the gravel alongside the pavement flying, and plastered Hattie against the leather interior. A glance over revealed one of her hands still clutching the belt crossing her chest and her eyes wider than silver dollars. He stifled a chuckle, enjoying the wind through his hair and look on her face.

About a quarter mile up river, he made a quick right turn onto the Heton bridge, and another right, then continued in the direction from which his passenger claimed to come. The rarely traveled and rutted frontage road shook the vehicle's suspension, while tall grass rubbed against his shiny paint job. He gnashed his teeth together, gripping the wheel so hard his knuckles whitened. He should have made the confused wench walk. If this so much as scratched his car....

Appearing less stressed, but still clutching the

armrest, Hattie leaned forward in her seat and peered through the windshield. Her gaze occasionally bobbed back to the vette's interior, arching a brow at the knobs and gauges on the dashboard, then back to an intent stare on the empty and overgrown road. "I don't understand. We should see the wagons by now."

"Maybe we haven't driven far enough." Case humored her, not knowing what else to do. He eyed the cell phone on the console and considered calling 911. If they didn't find the wagons she insisted upon, what mood would he face then? Was she going to become more hysterical and less manageable? Only someone a little daft wouldn't recognize a 'vette when they saw one.

"Oh, Lord." Hattie buried her face in her hands and began sobbing.

Case stopped the car and swiveled in his seat. "What's wrong?"

She straightened and peered at him through teary eyes. "I'm so confused. We should have come upon the train by now. I can see for miles ahead, and there's nothing there. This road hasn't been traveled for ages. Billy said this is the way the last wagons came, so I don't understand." She collapsed into tears again.

"Don't cry." Case gave her shoulder a tentative pat. "I think I should take you to my house and let you get some rest. I'm sure my mom has something that'll fit you so you can get out of those damp clothes, and perhaps we can make some phone calls and straighten out this whole mess."

Confusion clouded the stare fixed at him before she lowered her face into her hands again, her wailing louder than ever.

"What'd I say?" He released a huge breath.

"I don't know what a phone call is." Her face still covered, her muted words were barely audible.

Lord, what had he gotten himself into? She claimed no knowledge of a car, now a phone, and she dressed like someone straight from the streets of old Tombstone. He splayed one hand through his hair. Years had passed since he needed his mommy, but boy did he now. He surveyed the area and slapped his forehead. How did he get off this narrow river road without doing any more damage to his car? "Crap," he muttered.

He drove a few feet further to a wider spot and, jockeying back and forth, managed to make a u-turn. He paid careful attention to the dirt trail but, with his peripheral vision, watched his passenger. Her shoulders quivered with each sob, and despite wanting to forget he'd found her, her emotional state worried him. Had she escaped from a mental facility? Surely, no one wanted to be seen dressed like someone from Annie Oakley's era, and her story about a wagon train made no sense. No one in their right mind would believe her.

The hair on the back of his neck bristled. He needed advice, and quick. Luckily his family home wasn't far away. Turning back across the bridge, the Corvette glided onto paved road and picked up speed. Case's relief released in a sigh.

At this time of year, the scenery looked the same no matter which way you looked: rows of corn growing for miles. Hattie straightened in her seat and struggled with the wind battering her bonnet. She eventually removed her head covering, freeing her long tresses to whip about her face. She swiveled her gaze from side-to-side, but remained silent.

Among a sea of green stalks, Case spied a large white mailbox and steered onto a graveled road. "There's my house." He pointed ahead then stopped in front of a gate.

Hattie swiped her wayward hair behind her ears and craned her neck up at a large, white two-story. Even the Franklin's impressive home didn't rival this one set amidst tons of trees, some evidently generations old. A huge grassy yard rolled to meet all the different colored roses blooming on bushes planted along a split-rail fence. "It's beautiful." She gazed through red-rimmed eyes at Case but went back to staring at the house.

"The barn over there," he pointed to the left" houses all the farming equipment and," and he pointed to the right, "the stables aren't as full as they once were, but we still have a dozen or so horses raised for stud."

Not young and naïve enough to lack understanding, her cheeks heated. She'd seen horses mate before.

"What a beautiful porch." She changed the topic to the stylish overhang running the length of the house. Twin rocking chairs sat side-by-side, close to the front door—all so brightly white, everything looked freshly painted.

Case left the car, walked around to Hattie's side, and opened her door. "Welcome to the Atkins Ranch."

"Case." The front door stood open, and a slim, gray-haired, older woman, dressed in pants, called and waved from the porch. "I worried about what kept you. Did you get the bread I sent you for?"

"Sorry, Mom, I didn't make it to the store. Instead, I came across a young lady who needs our assistance." He took Hattie's hand and helped her stand.

She smoothed her wrinkled and still damp skirt, managing a smile at Case's mother despite the unfeminine shortness of the woman's silver locks, and her shameless wearing of pants. A simple white top showed bared arms and revealed way too much throat to suit Hattie. The letter "J" hung from a golden chain around a wrinkled neck and sparkled in the sunlight.

Case placed his hand in the small of Hattie's back and ushered her through the front gate and up a strange, hardened walkway. She knelt and felt the surface, rising to meet his mother's extended hand. "Hello. My name is Jane Atkins. Welcome to our home."

Friendly demeanor aside, the woman's sweeping gaze of Hattie produced a definite raised brow to match her confusion and show a marked resemblance to her son. Why did everything look so strange...seem so different?

"Thank you, ma'am." She bobbed a curtsy, dipping her chin at her state of dishevelment. I...I—"

This is Hattie Carson, mother. She's had quite an

experience. Somehow fell in the river, managed to get out, and seems somewhat confused about what's happened to her. I thought perhaps some rest and a visit to the doctor might be helpful."

Hattie fixed Case with a shocked stare. "I don't need a doctor. And as far as being confused, I know perfectly well what happened, I..."

Jane Atkins fingered Hattie's dress. "You're still wet. Let's get you into something dry. Even though it's warm, we don't want you catching a chill. Won't you come inside?"

Hattie, reluctance tugging at her feet, entered the door Case opened. Her breath escaped in a rush at the opulence inside. The shiny entry she stood in ended with a rug covering the entire floor of a splendid setting room. Furniture in a style she'd never seen graced the area below a huge picture of curling waters slapping at flat land that sparkled like tiny pieces of glass. A bouquet of nature's beauty, arranged in a red and gold vase, sat on a long, low table in front of an extremely large settee, and delivered a heady aroma of sweetness into the air. She breathed in the scent and gaped at her surroundings.

"Come with me, my dear." Case's mother summoned her towards the staircase.

Hattie followed, climbing padded stairs, her gaze still wide with wonder, and then entered a bed chamber that made her gasp. Bright light filtered through slatted window coverings onto a bed big enough for half the orphanage to share. The floral spread and massive fluffy pillows made her want to jump into the midst of the apparent comfort and wake from the nightmare that had become her life.

Mrs. Atkins went to a set of doors and opened them wide, revealing a hidden room, that like Abby's armoire, held a mercantile's worth of dresses. Jane picked through the masses, finally plucking one from the bunch. Turning, she held up a long gown made of a shiny fabric. "This silk robe should work until we launder your...your dress and undergarments. Tell me, dear, is that some sort of costume?" She shoved her selection at Hattie.

Costume indeed? She dipped her chin. Abby had given her this fine dress. What would Case's mother think if she'd seen the clothing Hattie had worn at the orphanage? She shuddered at the thought. Ignoring the insult, she accepted the flimsy gown. "Thank you, ma'am."

Case's mother pointed toward an open door. "There's the bathroom. Feel free to wash up, shower, or whatever you'd like. My comb and brush are on the counter. Make yourself at home, sweetheart. I'll be downstairs. Join us when you're done, won't you?"

Jane left, leaving Hattie alone. She clutched the silken garment to her chest and stood in the middle of the room, afraid to move. Had the cold water shocked her system? Everything around her made no sense. A large square box made of glass, hung over a marbled fireplace, a strange handless clock, showing only numbers rested atop the short table next to the bed, and tintypes of other folk, all strangely dressed, hung on the walls. And what of the cool air blowing down on her from overhead? Goosebumps raised on her arms.

Sensing for the first time, her wet feet, Hattie bent and unlaced her boots and removed them and her damp stockings. Placing them on the hearth, she wriggled her toes in the plush floor covering, marveling at the softness caressing her feet. She stooped and splayed her fingers through the rug and wondered what made it so lush. Was this a dream she'd awaken from and find herself on her pallet in the wagon? A smack of her cheek didn't transfer her back to her roots. Her mind spun with confusion. What was this place and how had she gotten here? She summarized the day's events and muddled her mind further.

Bathroom? The word replayed in Hattie's mind and piqued her nosy side. Forcing herself to move, she entered the open door and stopped dead in her tracks. She stiffened, her mouth agape. A tub, larger than she'd ever seen, stood against a far wall, surrounded by plants, candles, colored bottles, vials, and tubes.

Nearby, was the counter Jane had mentioned, with more bottles and jars, plus two bowls sunken inside the glossy surface. Her bewildered gaze stared back at her from a mirror covering the entire wall. She frowned at her shabby appearance and understood why Jane wondered about Hattie's clothing.

Along the other wall, sat a little covered seat, strangely shaped, and when opened, displayed water colored a deep blue. A small shiny handle, similar to the one on the conveyance Case called a car, decorated the cool surface. She pressed down on the lever and jumped back, watching the liquid inside the bowl-shaped chair swirl like the river current that'd swept her away. With a gurgle, the water emptied, immediately refilled, and once again turned the color of a winter sky. Hattie clasped her throat, and stared through disbelieving eyes, wondering about the use of such a contraption. Could this be part of a water closet she'd heard about from the Franklin's nanny? An indoor replacement for the privy? If so, what was the square room in the corner with the glass door and more shiny handles?

Hattie tested a similar looking one over a sunken bowl on the long counter. Water appeared, cold and constant. She raised a brow at the 'C' on the handle, then turned it off and tried the one marked 'H.' Hot water poured forth, steam rising in the air and gathering in a mist on the mirror. She tested the heat with one finger, jerking back at the burn. How could all this be happening? What explanation could she fathom? Nothing came to mind except worry over Billy and what had happened to the wagon train. How could the entire thing have just disappeared?

Worried tears blurred her vision. She gazed again upon her reflection, realizing the Atkins awaited her downstairs. She eyed the gown draped across her arm and viewed her rumpled image in the mirror. Although she doubted an intrusion, she closed the bath door and with nervous fingers, fumbled with the buttons on her bodice and yanked her dress over her head.

Amazed at the instant hot water and the fragrant lather from the bar of soap next to the basin, she washed her face, hands and arms. Standing clad only in her chemise, discolored by river water stains, she clamped her eyes shut to mask her nudity and discarded her undergarment as well. Without peeking, she slipped on the borrowed gown, allowing it to shimmy down her body in creamy ripples, the material soft and molding against her skin.

Hattie opened her eyes and gasped. Her cheeks flushed scarlet in the mirror. Every curve and outline of her body showed through the rose-colored gown. She'd never worn anything quite so revealing. Did Mrs. Atkins truly expect her to make an appearance in the parlor dressed so scantily?

Pondering her dilemma, Hattie picked up the hairbrush and drew it through her long tangles. The stiff bristles smoothed her natural curl and added shine to her hair. Amused at seeing so much of herself displayed in the large mirror, she smiled. Other than a reflection in the Mississippi River, the mercantile window, or the first complete glimpse of herself in Miss Abigail's mirror, she'd never surveyed so much of herself. Modesty ignored, she turned first to the left and then to the right, examining and finding pleasure in her looks. If anyone asked her opinion, she'd have to say she'd definitely matured into a fine-looking young lady.

* * *

Hattie descended the stairs on silent feet, her knuckles white from holding tight to the banister with one hand and her other fingers entwined in the bodice of the clingy gown she wore Her gaze roamed the smiling faces framed on the adjoining wall. Voices sounded from the living room, and upon reaching the bottom landing, she hung back in the hallway, cowering unseen, her modesty challenged and her mind a whir.

"She actually thinks she was on a wagon train?" Jane's voice registered surprise. "Do you suppose she was smoking those funny cigarettes?"

Smoke? Hattie's jaw tensed and she pressed her hand to her mouth. She'd never smoked anything in her life. Ladies just didn't do such things. The thought of carrying a tobacco pouch and papers in which to roll the dried leaves caused a bitter taste in her mouth. She craned her ear toward the parlor, awaiting Case's response.

"I'm not sure what her problem is, Mom, but I'm

pretty certain she actually believes her story. I didn't know what else to do, so I drove her back toward where she thought the wagons should be. Probably scratched my paint job too. That stupid road hadn't been used forever. She may be a looker, but I think she's got some serious mental issues."

"Well, what do you think we should do with her?"

Feeling like an interloper, Hattie fought bursting into the room and protesting her sanity. If not so confused about all the recent strange events, she might have, but in all honesty, she had no explanation. What did Case think? She inched closer to the doorway.

"Maybe we need to take her to a doctor or just call the sheriff and have him come get her. She's cute and all, but the last thing we need to do is saddle ourselves with a crazy person."

So he did think her daft. Her jaw dropped open for a moment, but she quickly composed. Her shock and angry became a tenseness in her shoulders. How could she lay blame? If only the wagons had been where she supposed they were. But—

"Absolutely not, Case." Mrs. Atkins protested so strongly, Hattie's wandering thoughts stilled and she went back to listening. "We can't just toss out such a gentle person. If she's lost and confused, dumping her among more strangers will only complicate things. Let's call Doctor Evans and ask him to drop by and check her out. Perhaps a few days rest will help her recall the events that brought her here. I can't imagine how she ended up in the river."

"Well, maybe a few days could help her straighten out the facts." Case's reluctance faded.

Hattie's hand moved too slowly to muffle her sigh of relief.

"Is that you, Hattie?" Jane called.

Case peeked into the hallway. "What are you doing out here?" His gaze swept over her, and he smiled. "Don't you look different? Certainly better than when I found you. C'mon in and join us. Can I get you something to drink?"

Following him into the parlor and feeling practically naked, Hattie crossed her arms over her chest. She sat in the first available armed chair, her shoeless feet barely peeking from beneath the long gown. "I'd really like some water."

"Not a problem, I'll fetch you a glass. Be right back." Chase disappeared through the open door.

Jane moved to the chair opposite Hattie. "Did you

find everything you needed, dear? My dressing gown fits you well."

Hattie clutched at the clingy material and stretched it away from her bosom. "Yes, thank you. And I appreciate the loan of something to wear. My dress and chemise are still upstairs. I assume you have a washtub but I wasn't at all sure where you kept it. If you show me—"

"Wash tub?" Jane's brow rose drawing furrows to the peak. "The washer and dryer are in the laundry room."

"Dryer?"

Jane's eyes filled with concern. "Oh, my poor dear, your experience has really stolen your memory, hasn't it?"

Hattie shrugged. "I'm puzzled by everything. First the wagons are gone, along with my friends and traveling companions, then all this." She gestured around the room, her gaze focusing on everything strange and new.

Case returned, carrying a large glass and thrust it toward her. "Here's your water. I hope I added enough ice."

She accepted the frosty container, noting the small floating squares. "You have an ice house nearby?" How impressive was that?

The quick bob of his head and the widening of his eyes caused her cheeks to heat. Had she spoken out of turn?

"I-I got the ice from the refrigerator...rather the freezer." He cast a glance at his mother, his look one of a man seeking help.

He'd never know how much she understood his apparent confusion. She took a sip, frustration addling her brain and squeezing tears to the surface. Was there anything these people said, did or owned that made any sense at all? Sniffing back her emotion, she sat the glass aside, stood and paced. "Dryers, refrigerators, wash bowls that produce steaming hot water, a clock with no hands...I've never seen any of those things. You don't just forget such wonders. What's wrong with me?"

Jane rose and embraced Hattie. "There, there, sweet girl. I'd say you're in shock. If you didn't hit your head, the coldness of the water must have affected your memory." She held Hattie at arm's length. "Come upstairs and lay down for a bit. We've called our friend who's a doctor, and he'll be stopping by shortly."

Shoulders sagging and too confused to argue, Hattie followed her hostess upstairs and back into the massive room. Jane motioned to the bed. "While I get the guestroom ready for you, you curl up here and have a nap.

I'll wake you when the doctor comes."

Wordlessly, Hattie plopped on the bed's edge. Maybe if she slept, she'd awaken from this nightmare. She crawled to the middle of the mattress, gathered a pillow to her chest and, on her side, contoured her body to the downy contents. Jane twisted a long rod and closed the slatted window coverings and drew the curtains. Darkness shrouded the room like the confusion that hung like cobwebs in Hattie's brain.

Case's mother reached across and spread a light cover over Hattie, pausing to pat her leg. "There, now rest, and I'll check in on you later." Jane closed the door behind her as she left the room.

Hattie heaved a sigh and drew her cover up to her chin. Visions of Billy danced in her head and his smile beckoned to her. Images of the Franklins and their children flashed through her mind. All those people couldn't have been something her imagination conjured up. There had to be a logical reason for their disappearance, but whatever it was totally escaped her.

* * *

Hattie stood on the bottom rung of the fence

around the corral and stared at the assorted horses in the pen. A gentle breeze stirred her hair and co-mingled the smell of sweet grass with the odor of fresh manure. Seeing the Appaloosa in the corner sent a searing pain through her heart—memories of Billy. Had he been a figment of her imagination? No, her feelings for him were too real. Still, how had things changed so quickly?

Hard to believe that three weeks had passed since Case found her on the riverbank. Jane had treated her with such kindness and understanding, Hattie almost felt like she had a mother. Case had been a perfect gentleman, showing her around the ranch, explaining about his father's death from a premature heart attack, which more clearly explained why he still lived at home. She embraced his pain as her own, equating it to losing those closest to her.

Still, the mystery of how she ended up in a time so strange cloaked her. The doctor had recommended rest and time to heal what ailed her. Jane had assured Hattie did little but lie around, but nothing had changed. In fact, with nothing to occupy her mind, memories of Billy became more and more real. The logical side of her argued daily that she'd made the whole thing up in her injured head. Had she?

Lost in thought, Hattie stared across the open field beyond the fence, hypnotized by the swaying grass. A hand on her shoulder made her gasp. Her gaze jerked to Case's handsome face.

"Are you all right? I called out to you several times and you didn't answer." Concern furrowed his brow.

Heaving a sigh, she stepped down from the fence. "Sorry, I was thinking about my past...uh, I mean future." She brushed her wind-blown hair from her face and tucked it behind her ears. Tears blurred his image. "What am I to do? I've followed the doc's orders for over a month and I'm still the same. He has no idea why I still believe so strongly I came here on a wagon train, and neither do I. What will I do?"

Case put his arm around her. "You'll stay with us, of course. Mother has become really fond of you. I suspect she always wanted a daughter." He laughed, and dipped his chin, focusing his gaze on the ground. "I must admit I'd miss you terribly if you left."

Hattie swallowed hard. She'd become quite attached to him, too, but his admission warmed her cheeks. In between diminishing thoughts of Billy, Case's broad shoulders, trim waist, and the way his pants clung so alluringly to his long legs, provided a welcome distraction. For the first time, guilt didn't consume her at allowing herself to be honest. Who knew if Billy even existed? She certainly couldn't deny Case's existence.

Consumed by strange emotions and at a loss for words, she welcomed the sight of Jane on the front porch, calling them in for lunch.

"We'd better hustle," Case warned. "Mom gets her feathers ruffled if people make her wait."

He took Hattie's hand and hurried her inside. The same tingles she recalled from Billy's touch skittered up her arm and spread into her chest. Was she getting used to living with the Atkins? Was this where she really belonged?

* * *

With hands on hips, Hattie perused her clean bedroom, and inflated her chest with pride. The nightstands glistened from a thorough polishing, the bedspread had nary a wrinkle, and the vacuum-cleaner that continued to amaze her had left the rug's nap on edge, unmarked by even one footprint. Outside her lace-covered window, blossoms forecast the return of leaves and spring's bounty of flowers and fruit. The faint chirping of birds sounded beyond the glass panes.

A little over a year had passed since Hattie came to live with the Atkins. Time had flown, and she'd had no idea when Case brought her here, this would become her haven—her home. She lifted her left hand and gazed upon the engagement ring he'd given her on Christmas Day. She touched the gleaming stone with her right index finger to make sure she wasn't dreaming. Her thoughts of Billy and the Franklins faded a little more with each passing day, and like the history book she'd shared at the orphanage that still haunted her memories, those she previously considered as family became like characters she'd only once read about.

No one questioned her or pressed for answers she couldn't provide. Jane chalked up Hattie's knowledge of the old west as a prior fascination with history, and the assumption that a head injury had caused her to conjure up an unexplained past prevailed as the best reason for her strange recollections. Even she believed the doctor's final verdict.

A warm body pressed against her and arms wrapped around her middle. She jumped, but smiled at the familiar smell of spice and musk that was Case.

He drew her close and nuzzled her neck. "You

haven't decided you don't like the shape of the diamond, have you?" His breath warmed her skin.

She crossed her arms over his and absorbed the safety and comfort he brought. Leaning against his shoulder, she realized her heart beat in rhythm with his. "Of course not. I love everything about my ring, and I love you."

Case spun her around and covered her mouth with his, their bodies contoured together with perfection. She twined her arms around his neck, pulling him closer and sagging against him as his allure sucked away her resolve. Her lips parted for his probing tongue, and she tingled from head to toe. They were getting married in June, and she couldn't wait.

* * *

Hattie cleared the table while Jane loaded that fascinating machine she called the 'dishwasher.' So many strange gadgets to digest since that fated last day with the supposed wagon train: Case's bright red 'car,' the magnificence of relieving oneself inside instead of trekking to a privy, the magical songs played on the 'cell phone' Case carried in his pocket, and television...what an unbelievable miracle, that one. If only she could truly understand how someone could forget such wonders.

With so much to relearn, as Jane said, and all the places and things Case had shown Hattie, she admitted her past recollections seemed more like something she'd dreamt rather than reality. She tucked the ketchup back in the refrigerator, still amazed at the bounty of food one could keep cold and fresh inside.

Jane closed the dishwasher door and twisted a knob on the front. The machine purred to life, leaving Hattie to wonder what went on inside amidst the splashing of water and all the whirring noises.

"Why don't you come upstairs with me. I have something I think might interest you." Jane's voice interrupted Hattie's musings.

She followed behind the woman she viewed as the closest person she'd ever had to a mother, climbed the stairs, and stood with curiosity gnawing at her while Jane tugged on a rope hanging in the hallway outside Hattie's bedroom. A ceiling door opened, and as if by magic, a second set of stairs appeared.

Jane turned and smiled, and must have noticed Hattie's perplexed look. "This is the attic...where we store things."

"Oh." Hattie had never seen one before...at least if the orphanage had an attic, she wasn't privy to it. There she went again. She made a mental adjustment before speaking further. There was no orphanage.

Jane climbed the first two wooden steps and glanced over her shoulder. "Come on up, but be careful...and, excuse the dust. I haven't been up here for quite a while."

Hattie scaled her way to the top, surprised at the size of the dim room she found and the amount of treasures there. Chairs, tables, boxes, a dressmaker's form, an old bed frame, and a few steamer trunks, as Abigail had called them. Jane flipped a switch on a far wall and an overhead light brightened the area. The age of many of the stored items now became apparent.

Jane drew a line in the dust coating a well-used table, then brushed one hand against the other. "I really should get rid of most of this stuff, but I just can't bring myself to let it go." She ran her hand along the marred headboard. "Take this for instance. This is the bed Case's father and I shared when we first married." Her eyes hazed over.

Hattie understood. Even cherished memories

caused pain. The ones she carried of those she now considered imaginary had brought her aches often enough. So why then did they still seem so real? No use asking the same stale questions. "What was it you wanted to show me?" She changed the topic, hoping to lighten Jane's mood.

"Of course, that's why we're here, isn't it?" Jane knelt in front of one of the trunks, this one plastered with all sorts of words and names that made no sense to Hattie. Where or what was 'Sweden?'

"The other night," Jane said, while sorting through the contents, "when we talked about your...your past, I was reminded of the journal I've kept for all these years. I thought you might like to read it since you apparently have such a strong love of history."

"Whose journal is it?" Hattie stepped forward and gazed inside at folded dresses, scarves, an old doll, and some baby shoes. A musty smell lingered in the air.

"I'm not sure I really know. I only read the first couple of pages and that was years ago. I always meant to get back to it, but..." She found the crinkled leather book beneath an old jacket and handed the thin ledger to Hattie.

"May I take it downstairs with me?" Hattie flipped open the cover and eyed the scrawled writing. Age had yellowed the pages and turned them fragile. "I'll be very careful with it."

"Of course, dear. Take your time, but you'll have to share what you read with Case and me. I think there may be an important bit of our past there." Jane chuckled.

* * *

Fresh from the shower and in her nightgown, Hattie shimmied between the silky-feeling sheets, turning to plump her pillows. The journal lay on the nightstand, and eagerness to read every entry pumped through Hattie's veins. In a few short months, she and Case would become man and wife, so what better way to learn about him and the Atkins' family? She did appear to love history...even copy it somewhat, as Jane and Case often corrected her language and chuckled at her strange habits.

Propped against the headboard and her downy headrests, she opened the journal's cover. Until now, she hadn't realized that several of the pages were missing and those remaining had been obscured by time and damage. The smudged ink made reading nearly impossible, and in some places, it appeared someone had spilled water on the pages and washed away entire thoughts and events.

Nothing hinted to the name of the owner. So much for discovering the identity she sought.

Flipping to a place where the writing became somewhat legible, Hattie read:

Today, I got me a job at the livery in St. Louis. The weather was hot and humid. I sweated so much, I must've worked off five pounds, which would be a good thing if I wasn't already skinny. The work is hard, but I ain't gotta pay for room and board. The man who hired me is letting me sleep in an empty stall.

Sometimes I get so lonely for family, I just wanna cry. Of course, men ain't supposed to cuz it makes them look soft. Maybe someday, I'll find a place to call my own and have a roof over my head instead of stars and tree limbs. I got me a new horse from the livery owner as my old one had gone lame and was plumb worn out. This job is bound to play out after a few days, so I got to find something else afore I run out of money. By my latest accounting, I have two dollars and forty-three cents. I'm plumb tuckered, so I'm gonna turn in for the night. It's hotter than Hades in this stable, but it's better than a poke in the eye with a sharp stick. I'll write more soon. WM

Hattie's eyes grew heavy from reading. She reluctantly closed the cover and put the journal in the nightstand drawer. "Hmmm, St. Louis," she muttered, as she flattened her pillow and settled down beneath the blanket. Coincidence? Maybe she and Case shared more in common than love.

Hattie stretched and turned out the light. Her mind raced, with thoughts of St. Louis, the orphanage, and Billy. Time had blurred his features and Case's came into view. Maybe everything had been her imagination—a result of her accident, but then…. A whole new crop of questions invaded her mind. Where did she really come from? Was Hattie really her name? What had caused her to fall into the river? Worn out from the onslaught, Hattie lapsed into a slumbering escape.

The morning sunlight beaming directly into her face woke her. Hadn't she just fallen asleep? She inched away from the brightness and rubbed her eyes, then stretched her arms high in the air. Her head ached from all the questions floating around inside, she supposed. Why did she continue to drive herself crazy, seeking answers that clearly she'd never find? As far as she knew, her name was

Hattie Carson and where she came from didn't really matter. Case loved her and anything important lay ahead not behind where her recollections might not even be true.

Slipping from beneath the covers, she planted her feet in the plush carpeting. Memories, seeming oh so real, rushed back of times she'd risen to the cold plank flooring of the orphanage, waking in a room where light failed to shine except for when the tattered curtains were open. Visions of a bright sun, rising above a distant horizon, tinting the sky in shades of orange, and blazing through the back of a wagon's canopy, played in her mind. How many times had she viewed that sight when the train broke camp and started an early morning trek west? She rubbed her temples and grimaced. How could all those memories be false?

With a sigh, Hattie stood and plodded to the bathroom. Pushing past recollections to the back of her mind where they belonged, she brushed her teeth and hair, and wondered if Case was up yet. He'd joked with her about being a time-traveler, and although he had to explain the meaning, she knew why he laughed at such an absurd idea. No one propelled through time. Did they?

CHAPTER THIRTEEN

Hattie snuggled back in her bed, tired from a day of helping Case with the horses. Feeding and grooming them usually fell to the livery hands, but he took great delight in caring for the animals. Joining him brought closeness only they shared, and she thoroughly enjoyed watching him exercise a few of the more spirited mounts. He had the knack. Sitting astride his favorite roan, he looked every bit the part of a cowboy. All he missed was the hat, as he dressed in something he called 'jeans' and boots for his stable duties. His dimpled smile melted her heart.

Jane had entertained several ladies in some sort of social which included a dice game. Bunko, Hattie had heard it called, but she avoided the house and skirted the possibility of questions for which she had no hard and fast answers. Now, bathed and in a fresh gown, she propped her pillow against the headboard and withdrew the journal from the drawer.

She thumbed to where she'd left off, careful of the fragile pages, and read:

I ain't sure who I'm keeping this here journal for, but I reckon I ought to apologize for not writing for the past few days. Tho I'm still here at the livery, scrunched down in my bed of hay and straining neath the lantern to see, this here job has ended and I've gotta find a new one or I'll be back out on the trail looking elsewhere. I ain't got much recollection of schooling but near as I can tell, my spelling ain't half bad, and I do remember Ma working with me on my reading and calculating. I shorely miss her.

Guess I best get some shut-eye so I can get up early and see if anyone is needing a good hand. Hope the good Lord blesses me. WM

Still not sleepy, Hattie's interest piqued at the young man's distress. Had he found work? She turned the page and continued reading:

Praise be. I found me a job. Today I met some fancy fella named Franklin at the local mercantile. Seems he and his family is heading to California.

Hattie dropped the book like it was on fire. This

couldn't just be a coincidence. She had to read more. Taking a deep breath, she picked up the journal and continued:

Been to Cally once, already, but I sure have a hankering to go back. I musta caught Mr. Franklin's eye when I rode by, as he signaled me to stop. Said he's needing a person to ride along, help with keeping his family safe and taking care of any chores that need doin. He'll supply the food plus pay me a fair wage soon as we get to the end of the trip. This is a way to a new start out west, so I'd best be snuggling down for the night. Will check in with him in the morning to see when he wants me to start. 'Spect we'll leave in a few days. WM

This couldn't be true. Someone from the life she swore she knew had written these entries. But what of the 'WM' at the end. Was that a clue to the person keeping the journal? In her present state, she couldn't read more. Her eyes were just too tired. Perhaps tomorrow, she'd ask Jane a few questions about where the journal came from and how she ended up with it. Tucking the book away, Hattie pulled her pillow down into place and rested her head upon it. The cool case soothed her cheek and reminded her that despite her beliefs of a life past, she no longer slept in a wagon on a feather pillow covered in a flour sack. Things had definitely changed for her.

* * *

Hattie stared into her plate. Fresh blueberries drifted off her waffle on streams of melting butter. She had no appetite this morning—just lots of questions.

Jane carried her coffee to the table and sat. She looked at Hattie beneath a furrowed brow. "Aren't you hungry, dear?"

Hattie put her fork down and leaned back in her chair. "No, not really, although breakfast does look delicious."

"Are you feeling well?" Case asked between bites. "You usually gobble everything down." He laughed. "I can't imagine how you stay so slender."

"I'm fine, really." Hattie took a drink of orange juice, wiped her upper lip, then placed her napkin in her plate. "I would like to ask a few questions, if you both don't mind."

Case pushed his plate to the side. "Ask away."

Jane nodded, dabbing her mouth.

"I've been reading the journal you loaned me, Jane,

and it's very interesting. Several pages are missing or damaged, so I wonder if you know who wrote it."

"Not really." Jane shrugged. "That old thing was given to me by my mother, whose mother gave it to her, and so on. I believe it was written by some long-lost ancestor, but for the life of me, I can't recall who." She tossed her napkin on the table and leaned on one elbow, her gaze vacant. "I'm sure Momma mentioned who wrote it, but I'd only be guessing at this point. I've always meant to read the journal, but until I thought of it the other day, I'd forgotten all about it. Why do you ask?"

"Just curious, I suppose." Hattie refrained from sharing her discovered similarities until she read further. As far-fetched as coincidence seemed, the entries could very well be. Besides, she knew no one who referred to himself as 'WM.' In a town as large as St. Louis, there were bound to be many men with Franklin as a last name. Her attempts to convince herself fell short and she longed to dash back upstairs to read more.

Case stood and pushed in his chair. "Are you ready, sweetheart?"

"For what?" Hattie peered up at him.

"Remember, we're going in to town today to look

for the perfect place for our wedding?"

Lord help her, she had forgotten. Lost in the past, she'd totally let today slip her mind. Delayed excitement surged through her, sending her heart racing. She leapt up. "Of course. I just got a little sidetracked, but I'm definitely ready to go."

* * *

Exhausted after exploring all of downtown Kearney for the perfect wedding site and finding a quaint little church she loved with a courtyard perfect for the reception, Hattie slid into bed, eager to read more from the journal. Her fingers trembled with the anxiousness she'd tamped back all day. True, she loved Case, but that didn't keep her from wanting to find out if she shared a connection with the diary's keeper. She found where she'd left off and read:

Hellfire! After eating at the saloon last night, I barely have enough money left to buy myself a plug of tobacco. Good thing I don't use the stuff. Saw Mr. Franklin outside his house. He sure does live high on the hog, but that aside, he tells me he's still got business to tend to afore we leave for California. I reckon I'll get my stuff together early in the morning and head over his way again. If he needs me to help get things ready, then I might earn a few extra bucks. Don't hurt none to ask. Oh, he told me he's taking along a cow just in case. Says he has three young uns and milk is mighty important for them. I admire a man who puts his family first. Wonder what his missus looks like. He sure dresses like a dandy. Didn't do much today, but I'm bushed. WM

Hattie rested the book on her knees and stared into space, her eyes wide. There were too many likenesses for this to be anyone other than the same Mr. Franklin who'd hired her. Bessie's frantic mooing echoed in her memory...the time Billy responded to the drunken cowboys shooting their pistols into the air. And the children? What were the chances the three this person wrote of weren't the twins and Zachary? She turned her attention back to the journal:

Today, I met Mr. Franklin's missus. She's a fine looking woman, but even better for me, I met the pretty young filly they've hired to watch over the children on the trip. I liked her from the minute I laid eyes on her and can't wait to get to know her better. She acts like a real nice girl, and I bet we share some common likes. I'm spending the night in the wagon outside the Franklins to guard the family belongings, and we're s'posed to leave at first light to travel to Independence and meet up with the rest of the trains. I got my eye on the window of a certain gal, hoping I might catch another glimpse of her. Dadgum oxen are right noisy animals. Two of them tethered right outside the wagon are bound to keep me awake, that is if I can sleep for thinking about Miss Hattie Carson. WM

Hattie bolted upright. The book slid from her lap and landed with a plop, on the floor. Confirmation! Her memories weren't made up! Torn between wanting to run and share the news with Case and his mother, she chose to keep reading. Her hands shaking, she picked up the journal and flipped to where she expected to find the next entry. A pang of disappointment gripped her when she found several more illegible pages. She thumbed through blurred ink and smudged paragraphs until she reached something readable:

Dang! I think Hattie is smitten with this deputy fella,

Tom. I'm trying not to be too bossy around her, but I'd really wish I'd asked for her hand so I could order her to stay away from him. He's like a hound dog circling prey he's treed. If shooting someone wasn't a hanging offense, I'd have put a bullet through him by now. Lord, I care so much for that woman, please help me to hold on to her. I want us to have a future together in California. WM

Captivated, Hattie clicked her fingernail against her bottom teeth. WM had to be Billy. Funny, she'd never put two and two together and figured out that the initials either stood for William or William Monroe. Billy was a nickname for a lot of men named William. Urgency drove her to learn more:

My prayers were answered. The deputy and his friends left today. The death we all assumed was murder turned out to be an unhappy gal taking her own life. I'm glad for two things, tho. One, we ain't got no killer roaming free amongst us, and two, Hattie don't seem to mind that Tom's gone. I think she likes me as much as I like her. I'm planning on getting down on one knee tomorrow. Would have today, but Mr. Franklin is a demanding taskmaster. He had me running in circles, milking the cow, searching for game, and greasing the wagon wheels. I'm plumb tuckered. WM

But Billy hadn't proposed. A knot formed in her stomach, and Hattie searched her memory for what kept him from asking that all important question. She had to know. She gingerly flipped another page, the old love for him resurfacing:

Today was Hattie's funeral. My heart is broken at losing the woman I wanted to spend the rest of my life with. I never even got to tell her of my love. I hope she knew of my feelings. Although we couldn't recover her drowned body from the river, the Reverend spoke over a marker I made showing her name and the dates of her birth and death. I wonder if I'll ever be able to live with the guilt that I lived and she didn't. I'm the one who told her to jump in and swim for safety. What I feared were Indians turned out to be only one who had strayed from his hunting party. We had a bit of a scuffle, but he high-tailed it away without one of us getting kilt. Part of me wishes I were dead. I don't know what Mrs. Franklin is gonna do without Hattie's help. The children already look like little lost sheep without her. I pray no more folks die on this trip, but in my heart, I 'spect there will be some who do. WM

Tears clouded Hattie's eyes. So she was considered dead and a mock grave left to mark her existence. Billy's entry supported her claim of why she jumped into the river, but what had happened to the wagon train? Why hadn't it been there when Case took her back to where she thought it should be? In fact, the entire area showed no sign of passage of any kind for months or even years. Instead of answering questions, the journal created more. What had happened to Billy and the Franklins? Did anyone survive the trip?

A revelation struck. She stared at the yellowed and aged pages. Though there were no dates anywhere, she'd finally come to grips with the fact that the present year was 2010 and these entries were from a time and place she knew too well. Through the insistence of others, she'd allowed herself to be convinced that some sort of injury had caused her to conjure up a previous life in the eighteen hundreds. Now she realized her past hadn't been a lie, rather real and documented before her. Vindicated, even more confusion embraced her now. She turned another page hoping for a peaceful and happy ending, but instead she found another great gap in time.

We're finally here. I totally forgot about this dadgum book, what with the excitement of getting to California and settling in to my new home. I couldn't bring myself to write after losing Hattie, but time has eased my pain, and she will always remain a dear memory. I had no other choice but to move on with my life.

The wagon train reached California on November 12, 1840. I was right pleased to get here. With Hattie gone, I pitched in and helped with the young uns as much as I could. Tending babies ain't as easy as it seems. Miss Abigail took Hattie's loss really hard, so much so that we had to ask some of the other ladies on the train to do the cooking while she took to her bed. We was lucky and got to Sacramento ahead of the heavier snow in the mountains. The weather here is mild. Not much more than fog and drizzle here most of the winter and the spring and summer weather was a lot more tolerable than in the south. WM

Hattie looked up and smiled. They'd made it. From

the tone of Billy's entry, they'd been in Sacramento for a bit. She couldn't stop reading now:

The good news is I'm gonna be a pa. I met Clarie Jo at a Sunday church service at Sutter's Fort. I wouldn't dare tell her, but she reminds me a lot of Hattie, has the same spunk, even the same sparkle in her eyes. She's a fine woman I love watching her belly grow big with our child. I secretly hope it's a boy so I can teach him all the things I wished my pa had taught me, but all I really want is for both momma and baby to be healthy. I know Clarie Jo is scared and wishes her momma was here, but Miss Abigail don't live far away and she's promised to come when its time. WM

Tears filled Hattie's eyes and spilled down her cheeks. Billy's heart belonged to someone else. Even if she could find a way to return to her previous life, she'd have nothing to go back to. Surely the Franklin's had moved on, found someone new to watch over the children and fill the gap left by her passing. Her heart ached until a realization drew her upright. She loved someone else, too. Maybe she was that time-traveler Case kidded her about, but her life was here and now. An explanation would be nice, but certainly not necessary. What she did need to know was how the Atkins family fit into the Monroe history? Was there more to the story than what Hattie had read? She so wanted to know everything that happened, but to what end?

Niggled with the need to share her findings, Hattie glanced at the clock and saw the time was well beyond midnight. Jane and Case most likely slept, but again, Hattie questioned what good sharing the recorded facts would do. Driven by the need to read more and unable to sleep, she picked up the journal, determined to ease her own curiosity. Though it pained her to think of Billy with someone else, she had to know about the baby's birth:

Lord be praised! I'm officially a father. James Case Monroe was born this morning at five thirty. He's a big boy and has all ten fingers and toes. Judging by his caterwauling, he's hale and hearty too. Clarie Jo did real fine, and she and the babe are sleeping. Miss Abigail spent the entire night, but the local doc got here to see to the birthing. She and my wife have become very close. I think Miss Abigail sees a little of Hattie in my wife, just like I do. As I sit here and gaze down on my son, I wonder how my life might be different if Hattie had lived. Though I loved her, I'm happy with Clarie Jo and even prouder she made me the pa I always wanted to be. I'll be a good one because I know what was missing in my own life. I'll make sure my son don't ever want for anything if I can help it. WM

Hattie closed the journal and stared into space. James Case Monroe? What were the odds? Case wasn't a common name; in fact, she'd wondered how he'd gained it in the first place. Reading more entries only raised questions that begged for answers…answers that changed nothing at all.

After turning out the light, she snuggled down in bed, drew the covers up and pondered her circumstances. With arms crossed behind her head, she stared at the moonbeams playing on the ceiling. Even if she proved the existence of the wagon train, along with Billy and the Franklins, and showed Case and his mother the entry proving she'd actually been alive in 1840, what did she hope to accomplish? She still didn't have answers for how she skipped years ahead, and now, there was no reason to try to get back. Besides, she honestly loved Case…and Jane. Life without them was unimaginable. Still, questions burned in her mind, and sleep evaded her. Tossing and turning, she tried to relax, but visions of Billy holding his new son kept playing in her mind. How did the name 'Case' connect the generations? The journal had ended with the birth of Billy's son...sort of like history's trail had grown cold.

The rising sun had pushed aside the moon and sent dim rays into the room. Still, Hattie hadn't slept. She stumbled from bed, her body tired from an uneasy night, and made her way to the bathroom. The mirrored image reflecting back at her almost made her giggle. Her hair, ragged from her fitful twisting, hung in snared tangles and presented a painful problem. Grabbing the nearby brush, a gift from Jane, Hattie drew the bristles through her locks, grimacing as she smoothed each strand. She'd barely finished when her full bladder reminded her of the reason she'd made the trip. The sound of another toilet flushing indicated someone else was up.

While she dressed, Hattie reflected on her new life. Surely, the Good Lord had brought her here for a reason, and who was she to question it? Jane had accepted her like a daughter, and Chase had fallen in love with her. Even more, she adored him. Maybe her time spent with Billy and the Franklins had been planned to show her that despite all her years in the orphanage, she *could* find a family and a fit.

While standing in front of the mirror and straightening her collar, she pondered the quizzical gaze in her eyes. Right then and there, she decided to keep everything she'd read to herself. A new life lay before her, and there was no use looking back since Billy and the others found the new beginnings they sought. She had too, only a little different than what she'd expected. The reflection she saw showed nothing but peace and happiness. Hattie ran a brush through her hair one last time, and following the aroma of bacon, went downstairs for breakfast.

Already seated at the table, Jane and Case smiled when she entered the room. Case stood and pulled out her chair. "Good morning, my sweet. Did you sleep well?"

"Never better," she lied. Traces of Billy she'd failed to notice in Case, surfaced like a bright sun over the horizon. His strong chin, his smiling eyes, the same stray curly lock that dipped low on his forehead—he definitely shared some of the same facial traits as well as an enormous capacity to love.

"Did you finish the journal, dear?" Jane asked between bites of toast.

"I did, thank you. It was very interesting. A relative, I

suppose might have been Case's grandfather thrice removed, kept a record of his travels. Although several pages were missing or damaged, I was able to learn he reached his destination safely. I'd love to someday discover more about your family."

"And maybe someday, you'll be able to recall where you've been and share the details with us." Jane smiled as she lifted her floral china cup to her mouth.

"Maybe." Hattie returned the smile. "Right now, I'm ready to make new memories. I'd love to have your help in picking out my wedding gown. What do you say?"

Jane's smile broadened. "Really? Oh, I'd love to go along, my dear. I have nothing planned for today. How about you?"

* * *

The air conditioning hummed steadily, cooling the overly warm June afternoon inside the foyer. Hattie waited outside the double doors leading into the church, surprised by how calm she felt. Breaking tradition, Jane waited alongside her, their arms clasped and both giggling like little girls. In the absence of a father, Hattie had asked her mother-in-law-to-be to walk her down the aisle, and she'd accepted.

The musical cue sounded and the doors opened. Hattie's stomach clenched. Case, standing with his best friend, waited at the altar with the preacher, while his cousin, Katrina, stood up for Hattie since she hadn't made any close friends since coming to the ranch. She had no doubt becoming Mrs. Atkins would resolve that problem. The small ceremony they'd planned had grown in numbers as every pew was filled. Strange faces turned as the audience stood, and Hattie clutched her bridal bouquet. Case's dimpled smile beckoned, and everyone else became nothing more than a foggy backdrop.

"Are you ready?" Jane grinned and tightened her grip.

Hattie snapped back to the moment. "Yes, yes, I am."

An uncommon peace and undeniable anxiousness urged her to sprint down the aisle. Instead, keeping time with the music she and Case had selected together, Hattie made sure to maintain a steady pace with Jane. Seeing her beloved warmed her heart.

At the altar, she handed her bouquet to her bridesmaid and clasped hands with her intended. The preacher's words faded into the distance as Hattie pictured the life on which she was about to embark. Case held her hands tightly, tears rimming his eyes but not dimming his smile.

"Do you Case Robert Atkins take this woman, Hattie Marie Carson, to be your wedded wife?" The mention of his full name drew her attention back to the moment. Case's "I do," came as no surprise. His love showed in his gaze.

"Do you Hattie Marie Carson, take this man, Case Robert Atkins, to be your wedded husband?" For a split second, Hattie swore she saw a misty image of Billy Monroe standing behind Case, nodding his head and giving her his blessing.

"I do," she answered without pause. In some bizarre way, she'd ended up with Billy after all...just generations apart.

Thunderous applause echoed in the chapel as the pastor pronounced them man and wife and the audience stood. The kiss that sealed their vows also eased any illusions Hattie had about where she was and how she'd come to be there. She was home at last, and ready to build a future with the man she truly loved.

The End

ABOUT THE AUTHOR

Ginger lives in TN with her husband, Kelly. She retired from her job at an institution of higher learning in order to move from California to be closer to her grandson, Spencer, who is the light of her life. (Shhh, don't tell Kelly.) Since her first release in 2003, she's signed over twenty contracts and is quite proud of her accomplishments. Although she writes cross genres, she counts anything set in the old west as a favorite. Still, if you ask her which book she's written is a true favorite, she'd have a hard time picking just one because she loves them all, as she hopes you will. You can find more about her and her work at: http://www.gingersimpson.com

ALSO BY GINGER SIMPSON
FROM BOOKS WE LOVE

Destiny's Bride
Ellie's Legacy
Betrayed
First Degree Innocence
Special Edition
Sarah's Passion
Sarah's Heart
Time Invested
Time Tantrums
Culture Shock
A Novel Murder
Ages of Love

ABOUT THE PUBLISHER

http://bookswelove.net

We hope you have enjoyed your reading experience. Books We Love and the author would very much appreciate you returning to the online retailer where you purchased this book and leaving at review. http://bookswelove.net

Top quality books loved by Readers, Romance, Mystery, Fantasy, Young Adult Vampires, Werewolves, Cops, Lovers. If you're looking for something spicier visit: http://spicewelove.com

www.ingramcontent.com/pod-product-compliance
Lightning Source LLC
Chambersburg PA
CBHW051016060726
47593CB00016B/399